"Are you say[ing I won't be] a good fathe[r?]"

Her head snapped back at his growl. Crossing one long leg over the other, she held her hands in a tight bunch on her lap. "Oh, come on. You're constantly traveling and your social life keeps at least three celebrity magazines in business. Are you seriously telling me that you have time to fit being a father into that schedule? That you even *want* to be a father?"

Irritation tightened his chest. She might be right about everything she said, but a sense of being cheated out of something he hadn't even begun to understand had him ask quietly, "And you think you have the right to make that decision for me?"

She grabbed her black leather handbag off the floor of the car and sat it on her lap. She lobbed her notebook into it and hugged the hard lines of the small rectangular bag to her stomach. "When it comes to protecting my baby, yes."

Dear Reader,

I had so much fun basing this story in London, a city I totally adore. I was born in London, and though raised in Ireland, I have a strong emotional attachment to the vibrant city.

I lived and studied there for a number of very happy years, and it's also the city where my mom and dad fell in love. They met in a ballroom in my Irish hometown, but my mom soon followed my dad when he moved to London, like so many other Irish people in the 1960s. My dad worked as a driver on a London double-decker bus, and my mum was his conductor! Sadly, they have both passed away, but I often think of them driving along Oxford Street together, falling in love and dreaming of a life together.

A similar dream to that of the central characters in this book, Lucien and Charlotte, who fall in love during a long hot summer in London. I hope you enjoy their journey.

My warmest wishes to you until we speak again.

Katrina

Their Baby Surprise

—

Katrina Cudmore

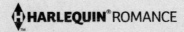

x

Recycling programs
for this product may
not exist in your area.

ISBN-13: 978-0-373-74442-8

Their Baby Surprise

First North American Publication 2017

Copyright © 2017 by Katrina Cudmore

Printed in U.S.A.

A city-loving book addict, peony-obsessed **Katrina Cudmore** lives in Cork, Ireland, with her husband, four active children and a very daft dog. A psychology graduate with a MSc in human resources, Katrina spent many years working in multinational companies and can't believe she is lucky enough now to have a job that involves daydreaming about love and handsome men! You can visit Katrina at katrinacudmore.com.

Books by Katrina Cudmore

Harlequin Romance

Romantic Getaways

Her First-Date Honeymoon

Swept into the Rich Man's World
The Best Man's Guarded Heart

Visit the Author Profile page
at Harlequin.com for more titles.

To Mom and Dad and the love you shared.

CHAPTER ONE

YOU CAN'T OUTRUN your past.

And right now Lucien Duval's past was staring at him from the radio studio's anteroom with as much warmth as a canister of liquid nitrogen.

That past being Charlotte Aldridge, the *verbal assassin* of Huet Construction's legal department.

Ten minutes ago, like an avenging angel to his guilty conscience, she had stalked into the anteroom, presumably sent to monitor every word he uttered in his early morning radio interview.

Ash-blonde hair coiled into a tight bun. Dark suit with buttoned-up blouse. Professional. Serious. A walking, talking, breathing human *Hands Off!* sign.

The type of woman he typically gave a wide berth to.

But those sea-green eyes of hers, which always observed him as though he was a disappointment, somehow also managed to burn something hot and liquid through his veins. Every. Single. Time.

And two months ago, he had learned that that tense mouth of hers was capable of softening and sending his pulse into another year.

And that those sea-green eyes, so cool and detached normally, could melt into a gaze of vulnerability and caution that had tripped over his heart. Two months on and he was still trying to shake off whatever hold she had on him.

The old scar just above his right ear began to tighten and itch.

He already had his board of directors haranguing him for his outspoken criticism of how the UK housing and infrastructure crisis was being managed—he didn't need the added disapproval of an employee he had recklessly slept with.

Charlotte had been an error in judgement, a slip in his usual strict self-control.

His honeymoon period as the new CEO and majority shareholder of Huet Construction was rapidly coming to an end. If he didn't start producing the results the City expected, the share price and investor confidence of one of the world's largest construction companies would soon be heading south.

And all of those who were sceptical of his buyout of Huet, who said he was an opportunist, a maverick, would be proved right.

Never.

He shifted in his seat; he needed to get out of this radio studio.

Now.

He didn't have time to be listening to yet more empty promises from a politician.

He had a gigabyte worth of emails waitin. him…and points to prove.

He leaned forward across the studio table a. growled, 'Enough.'

Mid-sentence, the Housing Minister, his fellow interviewee on the UK's largest breakfast radio show, leapt in his seat, his studio headphones twisting around, momentarily leaving him unable to speak as he tugged them back into place.

A quick look towards Charlotte's glacial gaze intensified his need to agitate, revolt, defy.

He switched his attention back across the table. 'Minister, I think you have bored the listeners enough, don't you? Let's allow them to enjoy their breakfasts in peace. It's the least you can do considering that the majority of them are actually having to live on a daily basis with the circumstances of this housing crisis: spiralling rents, the inability to provide a home for their families, couples unable to start families. And yet again, you're waffling and making excuses while not taking a single worthwhile action. When are you going to actually tackle the issues around land banking, compulsory purchase orders and the transparent disposal of public sector land? Look at innovative ideas like pre-fab housing? I say never because you have neither the courage nor the ability to do so. I'd have more faith in a bunch of toddlers with a box of play building bricks to sort out this crisis.'

With the minister grappling for words, an amused-looking radio presenter took the opportunity to wrap up the interview.

Lucien stood and approached the minister, who reluctantly accepted his handshake. Lucien gave him a brief nod and turned away. His plane was waiting for him at London City Airport.

Lucien swept through the anteroom and out into the corridor without as much as a glance in her direction.

Charlotte tried not to wince.

They had not spoken since their night together. It had been excruciating enough the few times they had passed one another in the corridors of Huet headquarters to nod in his direction, knowing what it was like to feel the weight of his powerful, hard body on hers, knowing the havoc his hands could cause.

But now, knowing that this would be the only time she got him alone, she chased after him as he strode towards the elevators. Instead of waiting for an elevator, he headed through the double doors to the stairwell so she followed him. Out in the empty concrete space she called to him on the landing below. 'Can I speak with you for a moment?'

He reached for the staircase handrail, looked at her impatiently and shook his head. 'I have a flight to catch.'

She dragged down the humiliation th.
wouldn't even afford her a minute of his time ɑ
into her stomach and followed him with resor
hardening her spine.

Struggling to keep up with him thanks to the
narrowness of her knee-length pencil skirt, she
called down to him, 'It won't take long.'

Now a full flight of stairs below her, he called
back in a bored tone, 'Speak to my PA.'

Cursing under her breath, while a new wave of
nausea folded her stomach into a cube of horrible-
ness, Charlotte yanked off her shoes and hoisted
her skirt. They had to talk. Now. 'I did yesterday
evening—she told me that you will be away on
business for the next fortnight.'

As he descended the last flight of stairs, she finally caught him up, with only the open iron ban-
nister separating them. He slowed and his eyes ran
the length of her bare legs. A surge of heat burnt
in his eyes. She dropped her skirt. She moved
down a step so that she was at eye level with him.
Six inches or so taller than her, he usually towered over her.

The last time they had been like this, at eye
level, was when they had been in his bed. When
their senseless rushed, frenzied, unexpected, kissing and touching and exploring in his garden had
been followed by him making the slowest, most
incredible love to her in his bedroom.

…it all been a dream?

…e searched his eyes now for some remem-
…nce, a hint that it too had been different for
…m…that she hadn't been just another conquest
of this renowned serial dater.

He blinked hard. Long dark eyelashes sweeping over narrowed, alert, brilliant green eyes.

A deep frown cut down through the centre of his tanned forehead, reaching the top of his perfectly straight nose. A nose at odds with the rugged handsomeness of his face, the thin line of his mouth, the boxer-like quality of the deep cleft in his chin.

Lucien carried himself with the street-savvy smarts of a man who had worked his way from nothing to being the CEO of a billion-dollar company. To not have acquired a broken nose or two on his journey from construction labourer to the majority owner of Huet Construction by the age of thirty-six proved his intelligence and shrewdness…and made the prospect of getting him to agree to her plans for the future even more daunting. He wasn't the type to roll over easily, but hopefully in this instance he'd be more than willing to see her head off into the sunset.

He came a little closer, his hand almost touching hers on the handrail.

Her heart kicked against her ribs.

His green liquid eyes blazed into hers, sending burning heat into her cheeks.

His gaze dropped to her mouth. Her lips, useless traitors that they were, parted.

A door banged higher up on the stairwell.

She jumped and he jerked away before making his way down the remaining stairs. 'Send me an email.'

She followed him out of the stairwell in her bare feet and ran after him as he swept out of the building, the receptionists and a group of visitors signing in, turning to stare at her.

Outside, seeing her opportunity to talk to him slip away, she reached for his arm and pulled hard.

He came to an immediate stop.

Eyes glinting darkly, he stepped towards her, lowered his head and murmured in that lightly French-accented voice that always managed to hold a sexy threat, 'I'm not interested in having a lecture on libel laws right now.'

His nearness, his voice, his warm breath tangling on her hair played dangerous games with her long-held resolve never to let a man get to her again.

She stepped back and prayed her cheeks didn't look as hot as they felt. She affected a laid-back air, in defiance of her galloping heart, refusing to bend to the blistering male chemistry swirling towards her. 'Well, that's lucky because I'm a construction lawyer, not a defamation one. I'll travel with you as far as the airport.'

'Didn't Simon send you?'

Simon was her boss. 'No. He did mention last week that he had threatened to send someone to monitor your interviews. So when my radio alarm woke me this morning to the news that you were to be interviewed alongside the minister, I decided it would be a good opportunity to get you on your own.'

A stalker alert flickered in his eyes. He stepped away. 'I have calls to make.'

A fresh wave of nausea hit her.

Maybe she should just leave it for now.

Get her head straight first.

But she needed him to know.

The only way she was going to get through this sudden turn in her life was by having a clear plan for the future. She needed certainty in her life.

If they had to do this on the footpath, so be it. But he couldn't leave without her personally telling him. She needed to keep him onside. 'I wanted you to be the first to know that I'm resigning from Huet.'

He gave an impatient sigh, called to his driver, who was waiting by the open rear door of a black saloon, to start the engine, and then shifted his attention back to her, '*Tu plaisantes?* You're kidding? Isn't that an overreaction to my interview? I wouldn't have been so easy on the minister if I hadn't been in such a rush for my flight. I know you legal heads are born pedantic worriers but you really need to relax a little.'

'This has nothing to do with the interview.'

Realisation dimmed his brilliant eyes to suspicious wariness. He walked to the car door and held it open, silently but grudgingly gesturing for her to get in.

His driver pulled out onto Regent Street and headed south to Oxford Circus. The stores on the iconic shopping street were still closed but the pavements were bustling with early morning commuters, coffees in hand, earphone leads dangling, heading to work. There was a buzz in the air; only now in late April were they having the first true warm days of spring.

He twisted to face her, drumming his phone on his knee like an insect at night tap-tap-tapping against a window pane desperate to reach the light inside. 'I take it that you're resigning because of our night together.'

She tried to stay impassive. She had been through worse. And survived. But having to share the most wonderful but scary news of her life with a man she barely knew had her rehearsed words stick in her throat and she only managed to eke out a pathetic, 'Yes.'

'I thought we had both agreed to put it behind us.'

Oh, God. There was no easy way to say this.

Get it over and done with. Then you can move on with your life.

A fresh bout of nausea joined her pounding heart.

The car was suddenly way too hot.

The panicked, terrified void that had almost consumed her in her doctor's consulting room reared up again. How would she cope? She couldn't possibly raise a child on her own. She knew nothing about child-rearing, being a parent.

And what if her depression returned? What would she do then? But it wouldn't. She was strong now.

And then there were all those selfish thoughts that had eaten her up with guilt: what of her aspirations to become head of Legal, to move into a larger apartment in London, to travel?

She gulped in some air and forced herself to look into those green heartbreaker eyes. 'I'm pregnant.'

He jerked away.

Behind him, they swept past Trafalgar Square.

Brow furrowed, he stared at her. 'Because of that night?'

'Yes! Of course it was that night. I wouldn't be here telling you if I had any doubt about that. I'm eight weeks pregnant—it has to be you.'

Lucien was once again tapping his phone against his knee, the silver case banging against the charcoal wool of his trousers. She had wrapped her legs around his that night, felt the hard muscle of his thighs. A night of insanity that had knocked her life completely off course.

Lucien shook his head. 'We used protection.'

She fiddled with the window switch on the door and lowered her window, needing relief from the heat rising in her. Not able to meet his eye, she muttered, 'Not in the garden…' She trailed off and looked at him, praying he didn't need further explanation.

He winced and looked away.

Lucien had held a reception in his Mayfair home for all of his HQ senior management on the night of his first AGM. Lucien's takeover of Huet had heralded a bonanza for the hairdressers and fashion stores in the vicinity of Huet HQ as the entire female workforce fell for his rugged looks and alpha charisma. But Charlotte knew a player when she saw one. And she refused to join his fan club. Having her heart broken once in a lifetime was once too often for her liking. No man would ever get the opportunity to do so again. In fact she went out of her way to ignore him whenever she saw him at work.

But a week before the party she had to meet with him to discuss issues on a bid contract. And, despite herself, his astute charm and lightning intelligence had threatened to melt her cynicism. At the end of the meeting, dizzy from the effect of being so close to him, she had almost tripped over a low coffee table as she had struggled to leave his office. While he had worn an amused lethal grin.

Brief glances were all they had shared the night of the reception. He had shown no interest in talking to her, and as the party had broken up she had gone out into the garden to find her phone that she'd left there, relieved to get away from her pretence that she was oblivious to him, but also a little miffed that he had spoken to practically everyone else except her. About to go back inside, she had felt her heart somersault when he had walked down the cobbled garden path towards her, his large frame even bigger as his shadow had moved towards her and engulfed her. She had offered a polite thanks and said she should leave with everyone else. But he'd told her that they were alone. Everyone else had already left.

He had smiled down at her. A kind, easy smile. A *Well, what will we do now?* type of smile. And she had foolishly stepped towards him, all thought and caution abandoned to that wonderful, what seemed sincere, glistening green gaze.

She had reached out her hand towards his open suit jacket with an unbearable urge to touch the dark grey material, to make contact with him.

And he had stepped towards her. Run his fingertips along her cheek.

And the next thing she'd known, his mouth had been on hers, hot, seeking, exploring.

In an instant her body had been aflame. His fingertips, his mouth, his scent, his hard, hard, hard body making her lose every inhibition, every memory, every protective layer she had grown over her heart and soul in the past six years.

Frenzied, they had unbuttoned and unzipped without thought, driven by a desperate hunger for one another. But when he had claimed her against that cold garden wall, she had stilled and her heart had gone into free fall. All of those memories of her ex's betrayal, of how lonely and ugly and beaten she had felt during her depression, had gushed back and threatened to drown her. Lucien had gently drawn away and watched her with a soul-destroying questioning, as though wanting to understand. Only after did it dawn on her that this was a key skill of any Lothario. The pretence to care.

But that night he had brought her to his bedroom and, her body weak with longing though her heart had been afraid, she had willingly gone. And he had made love to her, slowly and tenderly. And after she had cried in his bathroom when she'd realised how empty her life was…and how stupid, stupid, stupid she was to have slept with her womanising boss.

Now, as he faced the consequences of that night,

he ran a hand across the deep frown lines of his forehead and muttered, *'Zut!'*

Unexpected sadness pulled hard in her chest. A baby should bring joy, not this shock. What was he even thinking?

Did he hate her for this?

Bitterly regret the fire that had raged between them in the garden and the seconds when they had become one and senselessly forgot all thoughts as to the need to use protection?

Regret the baby growing inside her?

A fierce protectiveness surged through her.

Dismayed at how her hands were trembling, she pulled her notebook from her handbag and opened it to the pages where she had bullet-pointed her action plan. Needing the comfort of seeing in black and white her strategy for coping with this shocking but incredible turn in her life. 'My doctor confirmed two days ago that I'm almost eight weeks pregnant. My apartment here in London is too small to raise a baby so I've decided I'll move to the countryside, close to where my parents live. I will get work locally.'

He waved off her words with an impatient flick of his hand.

For five, ten, twenty seconds he stared at her intently, his gaze burning a hole in her heart.

He leaned a little closer, his shoulders tense, his eyes scanning her features like an interrogator searching for tell-tale body-language slips in a crime suspect. 'Are you certain that I'm the father?'

The lawyer in her knew that it was a reasonable question. But the woman in her, the mother-to-be, the idealist who believed in truth, fairness and honour, felt his question like a slap. She felt her throat constrict, a heaviness invade her sinuses, a burning sensation in her eyes. She was *not* going to cry. She was strong. A fighter. She sucked in some air. He was the serial dater, not her.

'I haven't slept with another man in a very long time. What happened between us was not typical for me,' she said fiercely.

She paused and cringed at having given him too much information and wondered why she felt she had to justify herself to him. Annoyed that she was doing so, she pulled in a steadying breath. 'I want nothing from you. I don't need financial support and I know a baby will not fit into your lifestyle. I want to give my child security and stability, a happy childhood. I've told you that you will be a father because you have the right to know but I don't *want* or *need* you in our lives.'

CHAPTER TWO

'I DON'T *WANT* or *need* you in our lives.'

Charlotte's words smashed into him.

His car, now opposite the entrance to the darkly historic Tower of London, was snarled up in a herd of London double-decker red buses and he had to rein in the desire to leap from the car and run. To run off the adrenaline twitching in his muscles, drying out his mouth, spinning his heart in crazy arcs.

He was going to be a father.

Something he'd never wanted to be.

Never wanting the responsibility, the fear of failing his child, never wanting to mess up, never wanting to have to face the fact that he was no better than his own father.

And he had always believed that a child deserved to be brought up in a loving environment with committed, responsible parents. Everything he didn't have.

But a failed, tempestuous, torturous marriage when he was in his late teens had proved to him that he was totally incapable of any such commitment.

And now, before he could even start to process

it all, to make sense of this turn in his life, Charlotte was trying to snatch it away.

Those sea-green eyes steadily held his stare when he looked back at her, the only hint of her nervousness in how she fingered the cream lined pages of her notebook.

He leaned a little closer to her. She backed away, her hand rising to touch against the edge of her delicate jawline.

Pain radiated in his own jawline, moving up through his clamped teeth and into his cheekbones. The scar above his ear throbbing, throbbing, throbbing. 'As you're pregnant, I'm going to ask you nicely to explain exactly what you mean when you say you don't *want* me in your lives.'

She recoiled a little at first but then sat more upright in her seat, both hands running over the material of her black skirt. She settled challenging eyes on him. 'You don't want to be a father, not with your lifestyle and commitments... Let's not get into an argument about this.'

'Are you saying that I wouldn't be a good father?'

Her head snapped back at his growl. Crossing one long leg over the other, she held her hands in a tight bunch on her lap. 'Oh, come on, you're constantly travelling, your social life keeps at least three celebrity magazines in business. Are you seriously telling me that you have time to fit being a father into that schedule? That you even *want* to be a father?'

Irritation tightened his chest. She might be right in everything she said, but a sense of being cheated out of something he hadn't even begun to understand had him ask quietly, 'And you think you have the right to make that decision for me?'

She grabbed her black leather handbag off the floor of the car and sat it on her lap. She lobbed her notebook into it and hugged the hard lines of the small rectangular bag to her stomach. 'When it comes to protecting my baby, yes.'

He inhaled a deep breath. 'Are you seriously saying that you have to protect this child from *me*?'

'Well, you're hardly "father of the year" material, are you? I don't believe for one minute that you really want the responsibility of a child.'

She had to be kidding.

'I'm a CEO of a company with a thirty-billion turnover, for crying out loud. Responsible should be my middle name.'

She gave him a satisfied look, the look of a prosecutor knowing they had caught the defendant out. 'Tell me, just how many companies have you acquired in the past ten years?'

He folded his arms. 'Sixteen.'

'And how many countries have you lived in?'

'What are you getting at, Charlotte?'

'The way you constantly move around the g...
is hardly the sign of a man able to give stabi...
and commitment to a child, is it?'

This conversation had gone too far. He leaned
closer to her and growled, 'Let me get this straight.
You want me out of your lives but yet are expecting me to blindly trust you in raising *my* baby?'

The words *my baby* leapt from his mouth unconsciously.

Charlotte looked at him aghast. 'I'll give *my*
baby security, routine. I'll be the best mother that
I can be.'

Beneath her defiant tone, there was a nervousness she didn't quite manage to disguise. Was she
as confident about being a parent as she was trying to portray? 'Did you want this—to be pregnant? To be a mother?'

She lifted one of the gold chain handles of her
bag, the only hint of flamboyance in her entire
wardrobe, and twisted it around her index finger,
the metal tightening as she twisted once, twice,
three times. 'Not until now.'

'Why?'

She gave a shrug. 'I was focused on my career.'

Dieu! This was such a mess. A thought tugged
in his heart and leaked out into his chest: this baby
deserved better than this. He needed to start fo-
cusing on the practicalities, understanding just
where they stood. 'Are you seeing anyone else?'

She eyed him warily. 'Why are you asking?'

He fisted his hands, a stab of jealousy side-swiping him at the possibility that she was dating someone. 'I want to understand who will support you.'

She unravelled the chain from her finger, in one fast, furious movement. 'You're the father. There's no one else in my life.' She paused and vigorously rubbed the red welts the chain had left. 'I know you might find all of that hard to believe given your social life, but it's the truth.'

He itched with the desire to reach for her finger and soothe her skin himself. That night she had touched him lightly, tenderly, almost reverentially with those delicate hands. That feather-light touch just one of the many inexcusable reasons why he had broken his own ethical code that he never dated employees, never mind slept with them. Exasperated at his own weakness and lack of honour that night, he said sharply, 'Don't believe everything you read in the media.'

She rose a disbelieving eyebrow. 'I saw a picture of you with Annabelle Foster online over the weekend.'

Yes, Annabelle Foster, a TV news reporter, had accompanied him to a Homelessness charity ball, but they had left early, his driver dropping Annabelle directly home. Alone.

Since his night with Charlotte he had dated a

few women, but he had ended each date early, a restlessness making his bones itch as he had tried but failed to focus on his date across the restaurant table from him, images of Charlotte's vulnerable, tender, passionate gaze when they had made love in his bed leaving him with no appetite. For anything.

'It's tiresome to attend functions on my own. I enjoy having company, but that doesn't mean it's anything more serious than a night out.'

She considered his answer with a suspicious frown but then, with an *it doesn't matter anyway* shrug, swung her bag back to the floor. She gave him the faintest whisper of an understanding sigh. 'I know this must have come as a shock to you. It did to me. But I want this baby... I want to give him or her the same happy childhood I had, with lots of love, laughter, happiness, certainty.'

All of the things he hadn't had as a child. Instead he'd had arguments and accusations and animosity.

The worst being the night he'd woken to hear his mother sob downstairs that she hated her life, hated being married to his father, hated being tied down with a child with no way out.

His father had lashed back demanding to know if she seriously thought he wanted any of this, a nightmare marriage, his dreams of university, of a better life, long abandoned as he was now straddled with a wife and child to support.

It was another four years before they divorced, five years until his mother eventually threw Lucien out for punching her new boyfriend. Her boyfriend had caught Lucien stealing his beer and had flung a beer can at him. Lucien, sick of the controlling bully who spent his days belittling his mother, had launched himself at him, long past caring about the consequences of anything he did in life. He had ended up with a permanent scar over his ear and living in a fleapit in Bordeaux at the age of seventeen. But at least there, there wasn't the constant silent, frightening tension of waiting for another bitter argument to start.

History could not repeat itself. This baby was never to feel unwanted.

That thought hit him hard in his gut, in his heart.

'So who will support you in raising the baby?'

Her arms folded tightly on her waist. 'My parents will be nearby. I know they will adore being grandparents.'

Which was something…but a feeling of loss, of not being in control of how his life was changing, of needing to make sure he got this right had him warn, 'Being a single parent won't be easy.'

She closed the window beside her and gave a shrug. 'I'll manage.'

But would she? He didn't know her, not really. For a few crazy hours he had experienced a connection with her that had flummoxed him, but with hindsight he had recognised that it had been nothing more than a mutual powerful attraction.

And now she was expecting him to be happy with entrusting her with raising his child. What was the best thing to do? For the baby? Neither he nor Charlotte mattered in all of this. 'Don't you think a child has the right to know its father, to benefit from that support?'

White teeth bit down on the soft, tender plumpness of her lips. He cursed silently at the drag of attraction that barrelled through him.

She pulled on the collar of her plain lilac blouse and eyed him impassively before she answered, 'Perhaps, but only if the father wants and is capable of doing so.'

Fresh irritation swept through him. He set furious eyes on her. 'You're making a lot of dangerous assumptions.'

She held his gaze, her mouth now a thin line of scepticism. 'Am I?'

'Let me be clear. I'll make the decision as to my role in this baby's life. Starting with understanding just how you propose to raise it. Are you going to work full-time? Who will take care of it when you do? Have you thought through the financial implications? Who else in your life will support you? What happens if something happens to you,

you get sick or are in an accident—who will care
for the baby then?'

'Nothing's going to happen to me.'

She spoke with a tremor in her voice. For a moment he paused, taken aback by the fear in her
eyes…the same fear and vulnerability he had seen
the night they'd spent together. Inexplicably he
was hit with the urge to reach out for her again,
to pull her soft body against him, to whisper that
everything would be okay. Just as he had done
that night.

Canary Wharf Tower, a touchstone for the com-
mand of commerce and finance in London, was
now visible in the distance. Until thirty minutes
ago he had thought of nothing but business and
stamping his mark as the most successful owner
in the global construction sector. He had worked
for almost twenty years to achieve that position,
moving from labourer to site management and
then into operations. Moving companies, moving
countries, working, working, working. Acquiring
small companies in the early days and rapidly and
aggressively expanding those by taking risks, all
the time defying economic predictions. Needing
to prove he was strong, that he wasn't a failure,
wasn't a coward.

The feeling that he was at a critical crossroads
in his life moved through him, dancing from his
whirling brain down to the confusion plugging his

chest. 'How can you be sure nothing will happen? None of us know what the future holds—you need support in raising a baby.'

She reached down for her handbag again and, placing it on her lap, searched through it, not looking towards him when she answered, 'I'm sure friends will help me.'

'And your parents?'

Her fingers clasped the sharp, firm ridges of her handbag bottom. She eyed him warily before mumbling, 'They'll be supportive but they're elderly.'

'Have you siblings?'

'No and I don't see what the issue is here. Lots of people are happily brought up in single-parent homes.'

'The *problem* is that I don't like being given ultimatums. I will decide what involvement I want, when I'm ready to do so.'

She turned to stare out of her window.

When they passed a signpost for the Docklands Light Railway, Blackwall Station, he knew they were close to the airport.

Her gaze fixed on the outside world, she said in a low voice, 'Even though I don't *want* you in our lives.'

He closed his eyes for a moment, her words stinging hard.

He was another mistake in a woman's life.

Too angry to speak, he willed away the remaining ten minutes of his journey.

He needed space and time to think.

He needed to get away from the woman next to him. The soon-to-be mother of his child. He see-sawed from an infuriation at her coldness, her icy assertion that she didn't want him in her life, to a deep desire to tug her to him and kiss away that frozen exterior to the warm, passionate woman he had spent the night with.

When his driver pulled up at the departure terminal at City Airport, he turned to her. His words were lost for a moment when he once again was pulled under by her fragile beauty: the pale skin over high cheekbones, the plumpness of her lips, the high arched eyebrows over sea-green eyes that mostly belonged to the Arctic Circle but occasionally reminded him of the sun-kissed warmth of the turquoise sea by his villa in Sardinia. 'What *you* want isn't important. I'll do what's best for *our* baby. We'll speak again when I return from my business trips.'

He jumped out of the car and stalked away but pulled up when he heard her call his name.

She stood behind the door he had exited, her hands clutching the frame. 'I'll still be handing in my resignation letter later today.'

He walked back to her and stared down into

those defiant eyes. She pulled the car door even closer against her body.

He leant down close to her ear and whispered words that came from the very centre of his being. 'Trust me, I'm not going to let you go that easily.'

Later that evening, Charlotte left the open expanse of the Thames river walkway in Bankside to scoot down Clink Street. The dark narrow cobbled street once again sent an involuntary shiver through her. Now a fashionable part of London, this historic area, famous for Clink prison, still held a hint of menace. And she loved it.

She loved all of London. It was why she walked to and from her work in St James's to her home in Borough every day. Her journey took her past Big Ben and the Houses of Parliament. Then the London Eye, the giant wheel always making her smile when she remembered her mum's terror when they had ridden it for her fourteenth birthday. And towards the end of her walk came her favourite, Shakespeare's Globe Theatre. The timber construction embodying the history that this city was steeped in and the determination of its people to continue its rich and vibrant culture.

And now she was going to have to leave all of this. Leave her apartment, leave her challenging but exhilarating work, leave this buzzing city. She was leaving for all of the right reasons, but she would miss this life she had worked so hard to achieve.

Lucien's question earlier that day as to who would care for her baby should something happen to her came back to plague her again. She yanked the strap of her rucksack tighter on her shoulder, her sports-trainer footsteps falling silently on the cobbled street. What if her depression did return? Not that he knew anything about her past illness.

A tight, tight, tight cord lashed itself around her throat.

How would she care for her baby if it did come back?

That's not going to happen. I'm strong now.

She passed a noisy popular fusion restaurant and looked away from the smiling and animated couples and large groups of friends dining there. They all seemed so carefree.

In her final year at university she had been sucked deeper and deeper into depression. Not that she had understood any of that at the time.

At first it had just been a feeling of being overwhelmed by her workload, her looming exams and the self-imposed pressure of achieving a first-class degree. Unable to concentrate, constantly tired, her mind swamped by a sense of hopelessness. She'd kept it hidden for months. Not wanting to be thought of as weak. Feeling a complete failure. Not wanting to be a burden to anyone. Eventually she had told her boyfriend Dan and best friend Angie. And had somehow managed to drag herself through her final exams.

On the night of her final exam she had told Dan once again that she was too tired to go out. To her relief, for once he hadn't become quietly irritated with her. But later she had changed her mind. Hoping that now that the exams were over just maybe she would be herself again.

With that glimmer of hope sustaining her, she had made her way to the riverside pub. And had found Dan and Angie in the beer garden. Kissing. Intimately. Lovers intimately.

Dan had been the first to see her. He had broken away and approached her with a guilty but almost relieved look on his face. Within minutes she had learned that they had been dating for weeks. And it was over between herself and Dan.

She had gone home to her parents that night. Broken. And had spent the following year slowly dragging herself out of the swamp of depression.

In the years since, she had wrapped up all the memories of that year into a tiny capsule that sat deep within her. Knowing that she needed to mind herself, protect herself against the depression returning. And she did that by telling herself that she *was* strong, protecting herself in relationships, and guarding herself against men who might hurt her again.

She passed an upmarket burger restaurant and walked on by. But a few steps on she came to a stop and turned around.

She needed a milkshake.

Twenty minutes later, she turned right onto Kipling Street, sucking hard on the thick sweet vanilla mixture, fears at bay for now, just glad to see her apartment block further down the street and the prospect of watching escapism TV for an hour.

The drink straw dropped from her mouth.

And her shock was much too quickly superseded by the hot heat of embarrassment and soul-destroying attraction.

Leaning against the door of this dark saloon, Lucien was talking on his phone. Earthy, menacing, sexy.

He hadn't seen her yet.

She pushed away the impulse to run away and instead put the milkshake carton in a nearby bin, tidied the strands of hair that had escaped her ponytail, grimaced down at her purple and blue leggings and dark navy sweatshirt, and tightened her grip on her rucksack handle.

He became aware of her when she was twenty paces away. He continued to talk on the phone but he watched her intently. Every. Single. Step. Of. The. Way. Green eyes narrowed, lazily travelling down her body and back up again.

He was tieless, top button undone, his shirt sleeves rolled up. His dark brown hair was cut tightly into his scalp at the side, the top a little longer and curling slightly, adding to his air of menace. The powerful strength of his fighter body was clear in his muscular forearms, the broad width of his shoulders, the long length of his legs, planted wide apart.

Lucien didn't look like the other suave CEOs that swarmed London. Instead he looked like a dock worker from Marseille who modelled and took part in mixed martial arts in his spare time.

She hated how attracted she was to him.

She hated how her body melted just seeing him, the tight longing that pulled hard within her.

She hated the physical hunger that froze her brain and all logic.

Destructive, crushing chemistry.

She came to a stop a few steps away from him and he finished his call.

They stared at each other and she raised an eyebrow. Determined not to be the first to talk. To ask him why he was here. To say that she thought he was away on business for the next fortnight.

His gaze dropped down along her body again. And stopped on her stomach. Heat blasted through her at the intimacy, protectiveness, ownership of his look.

Her heart thudded in her chest.

He was the father of her child.

They would be bound for ever.

A thought that was mystifying, incredible, terrifying.

She cleared her throat loudly and dropped her rucksack down in front of her, to swing against her legs. Her arms now shielded her belly.

'We need to talk,' he said.

She wanted to say no. This morning had been way more difficult than she had ever anticipated. In perhaps complete naivety she had thought Lucien would be shocked but accepting of her plans for the future. He wasn't father material, after all. She had sat at her desk all day thinking about what he had said. And come to the realisation that she needed to reassure him of her ability to care for their baby.

He gestured down the street. 'We can talk in a café on the High Street.'

'The smell of coffee makes me nauseous.' She hesitated for a moment as the lines around his eyes tightened. In concern or dislike at another reminder of her pregnancy? With a sense of inevitability and a need to get this over and done with, she added, 'We can talk in my apartment.'

Lucien said something quickly to his driver and then she led the way into the 1960s redbrick block.

Inside the foyer, he reached for her rucksack. 'I'll carry your bag.' For a brief moment their fingers met. Their gazes clashed and all of the intimacy, the intensity, the closeness of their night together rushed back.

She yanked her hand away and, not welcoming the prospect of being stuck in the tight confines of the lift with him, led him to the stairwell instead.

Walking alongside him up the stairs, she asked, 'What explanation did you give Human Resources for wanting my address?'

He looked at her with a hint of bemusement. 'The HR director has enough sense not to ask.' Then his features fixed back into their usual hard shrewdness. 'I also spoke to Simon. He made no mention of your resignation.'

They had reached the third floor and she paused on the stairwell and answered, not quite able to meet his eye. 'I didn't resign... I'll do so tomorrow.'

'Why?'

His now dispassionate tone, so in contrast to the heat of his gaze in the foyer, his lack of understanding of how her life was being turned upside down and his insistence on questioning everything she needed to do had her answer crossly. 'Simon was busy, and frankly I couldn't face it... not after this morning. I couldn't take another difficult conversation today.' She paused, and as the true realisation of what she was giving up hit home she grabbed her rucksack off him. 'I love my job.

I've worked so hard over the years to get to this position.' A lump suddenly formed in her throat. She knew of her reputation as a tough negotiator within the wider organisation, but within her department, where she was one of the most senior staff members and often mentored the younger staff, she was more relaxed, more herself. 'It's going to be hard to say goodbye to everyone.'

She twisted around and stormed through the door into the corridor that led to her apartment. As she searched her rucksack for her keys he joined her at her front door and said, 'You don't have to resign.'

'Yeah, that would work out just fine—me pregnant with the CEO's baby and we can't even bring ourselves to say hello in the corridors.'

'That's why I came back from Paris. We need to sort this out now.'

With tense fingers she opened the front door of her apartment, a heavy knot of anxious speculation landing in her stomach at his words, while simultaneously managing to worry about the trivial: what would he make of her minuscule apartment, especially in comparison to his vast five-storey Mayfair town house? But her love for her apartment's bright open interior and pride that she had finally managed to get a foothold on the crazy London property market had her march in ahead of him.

In the open-plan lounge and kitchen she gestured to her grey velvet couch, silently inviting him to sit, and asked, 'Can I get you something to drink?'

He didn't sit but instead paced around the room. The room shrank around his restlessness, the power and strength of his body. Needing some oxygen against the tension in the room, she moved to the lounge window and opened it to the still-warm April air.

When she turned back to face him, he hit her with a non-compromising stare. 'I want to be a part of this baby's life on a daily basis.'

The knot of anxiety inside her twisted. 'That's not possible, you know that. I'm moving away from London.'

'Don't move away.'

She gestured around her apartment. 'I need more space. I need to be near my parents. To have family close by.'

'I agree, that's why I believe you should move in with me…and, for that matter, why we should marry.'

She sank down onto the window seat below the open window. 'Marry!'

'Yes.'

A known serial dater was proposing marriage. This was crazy. He had the reputation for being impulsive and a maverick within the industry, but his decisions were always backed up with sound logic. And that quick-fire decision-making, some would even say recklessness, often gave him the edge over his more ponderous rivals. But he had called this one all wrong. She gave an incredulous laugh. 'I bet you don't even believe in marriage?'

He rolled his shoulders and rubbed the back of his neck hard, his expression growing darker before he answered, 'It's the responsible thing to do when a child becomes part of the equation.'

This was crazy. She lifted her hands to her face in shock and exasperation, her hot cheeks burning against the skin of her palms. 'Have you really thought about what it takes to be a father? A child needs consistency, routine, to know that they are the centre of the parent's life. Have you considered the sacrifices needed? Your work life, the constant travel, all of the partying—everything about the way you live now will be affected. Are you prepared to give up all of that?'

Standing in the centre of the room, he folded his arms on his wide imposing chest, his eyes firing with impatient resolve. 'I don't have a choice. This child is my responsibility and duty. I will do whatever it takes to ensure that it has a safe and happy childhood.'

'I can give my baby all of that.'

'You admitted this morning that you have limited support.'

'I have my friends.'

'Are they going to be there in the middle of the night when the baby is crying? Are they going to be there when you're exhausted, when you're sick, when you have work demands, when you need to be with your elderly parents?'

She flinched and lowered her head. Needing time to think.

Bitterly she accepted that he was right... She loved her two best friends, Tameka and Jill, both ex-colleagues from a previous employer, but she knew only too well the fragility of friendship.

When she'd had depression she had lost friends. Not wanting to be seen as being weak she had isolated herself, especially after Dan and Angie's betrayal, but also their reaction when she had told them about feeling down and unable to cope. At first they had been understanding and supportive but as the weeks had passed she'd felt their impatience, their nervousness. Their eyes had said, *Can't you pull yourself together?*

She stared down at the floorboards she had lovingly painted a pale pink last year, emotions sweeping through her.

Anger at those memories, anger at him for hitting so many raw nerves.

Frustration and guilt at being so daunted at the prospect of being the sole carer for a newborn, at the years that stretched out before her, knowing she was the only person protecting this precious life.

Fear about what would happen if her depression returned.

Anxiety about her parents' slowly declining health.

Perplexity at how stupidly attracted she was to this heartbreaker.

Overloaded with all of those emotions, she rounded on him. 'And are you going to be there in the middle of the night, when I'm exhausted, or are you going to be away travelling or out on a date?'

His expression tightened and he tilted his head back defiantly. 'I *will* take my marriage vows seriously, including to be always faithful.'

The absolute resolution in his voice, the deceitful, guilt-inducing thrill in her heart at his words, blew her usual coolness even further out of the water. 'Oh, please! You? Celibate? Are you kidding me?'

Heat entered his eyes, pinning her to the seat. 'Who said anything about being celibate?'

She leapt up. 'No way are we sleeping together again.'

He walked across the room and right up to her, inches separating them. He stared down at her, his eyes dangerously challenging her, daring her to lie about the attraction whistling through the air in the room. 'Why?'

He spoke in a low whisper.

She swallowed hard, a shiver running through her. 'Because you're not my type.'

'Which is?'

'A serial dater who probably gets a kick out of breaking women's hearts.'

A dangerous spark lit up in the corner of his eye. He moved even closer. She willed herself not to lean towards his heat, his gorgeous faint-inducing scent of leather and soap, his invisible pull that yanked on every cell in her body.

'Afraid I might do the same to you?'

She stepped back. Away from his power. 'No! Let me set you straight…my career and now my baby are all that matters to me. I don't have time or interest in relationships.'

'Good, so a working marriage will suit you perfectly.'

'A working marriage?'

'Think of it as a business relationship. We'll both be clear that the only reason we're married is for the welfare of *our* baby. Our mission will be to nurture and protect our child by working closely together and supporting each other in parenting him or her. It will be a team effort.'

He made it all sound so simple and logical. She shook her head and walked away, towards the kitchen counter, muttering, 'I think I'm in a nightmare.'

'This is the best solution. Our baby will have both parents in its life, you get to stay in London, stay working in the job you obviously love.'

Why was he doing this? There had to be more reasons than just because he felt responsible. Why would a player, a man known to live for his work, be willing to change his life so much when he didn't have to? A horrible thought took hold. Was this proposal nothing more than appeasing his board and protecting his reputation? It wouldn't look too good for a CEO to have got an employee pregnant. Even if he was the majority shareholder in the company. With a bitter taste in her mouth, she asked, 'Do you want to marry so as not to damage your reputation?'

He considered her with amusement, a faint smile on his lips. 'My reputation! *Je m'en fiche complètement!* I couldn't care less. I'll happily tell people that it was an accidental pregnancy and we decided to marry in order to raise our baby together. There is no shame in either. We're simply being responsible and mature parents.'

Her mouth dropped open. 'You'll do no such thing.'

'Why?'

'My parents are elderly and conservative…they believe in the sanctity of marriage. They would be deeply upset if they knew I didn't marry for love.'

Lucien threw his eyes upwards.

She eyed him angrily. 'My parents have the most wonderful, loving marriage imaginable. Just because you're totally lacking in any romance doesn't mean that it doesn't exist for other people.'

'Don't tell me that *you* were waiting to be swept off your feet.'

She fixed him with her iciest stare. 'Hardly.'

He looked at her warily. 'Do you want romance, love…all of that fairy-tale stuff?'

She folded her arms and threw him an unimpressed look. 'And here I was thinking all Frenchmen were romantics.'

'A lot of us are grounded in reality.'

'You're so grounded I can practically see roots emerging from your shoes. To answer your question, no, I don't want romance. Thanks to a few too many run-ins with men like you, I've been cured of all such desires… What my parents have is unique, but certainly not for me.'

'Good, so there's no reason why we shouldn't marry. My PA has set up a meeting for us at the marriage registrar's office tomorrow morning to give notice. You will need to bring your passport and proof of address. She also provisionally booked a slot for us to marry there in a month's time.'

She swallowed the yelp of disbelief that barrelled up inside her. And fixed him with a deadly stare. 'Wasn't that a tad presumptuous on your part?'

'Simply forward planning in the knowledge that your logical legal brain would see the sense of this plan. We have only seven months to get to know one another, to establish an effective working marriage. I want any potential issues resolved before the baby arrives.'

His words should have brought comfort; what he was proposing could, just maybe, work…on paper. Her baby would benefit from having another person in his or her life.

But what if Lucien proved to be unreliable?

And what of her attraction to him, how vulnerable she already felt around him? How she was always waylaid by her attraction to him, abandoning logic and self-preservation to the sound of his voice, the sight of his rugged face, powerful body, the pull of his clean, masculine scent.

She paced the room.

Dizzy, overwhelmed, giddy.

She had to think of her baby. And one thought kept snaking around her brain, around her heart. What if her depression returned? Who would take care of her child then?

She went to the kitchen counter and poured a glass of water.

The cold liquid calmed the nausea swishing around in her belly. 'Do you mean it when you say that it will be a business relationship and nothing more?'

'Let's call it a team effort—we will raise our baby together and support one another at home and in our careers.'

His voice was calm, conciliatory, at peace with the decisions he had taken. A red rag to all of the fears coursing through her. 'But will we be a team…or are you expecting me to make all of the changes? It's me who has to leave my home, my independence. The plans I had already made for our future, the baby and me. Will you accept my desire to have a career of my own? Will you accommodate my friends, my parents, my interests? Or will I have to flex to your way of life? Will you change the way you work, your socialising? Will you welcome me and the baby into your life or will you always begrudge us?'

She had spoken angrily, her fear sitting at the base of her throat. She expected him to respond just as angrily but instead he walked towards her. He held her gaze while gently fixing a loose strand of hair behind her ear. 'I will never make our child feel unwanted.'

His expression grew even gentler; concerned eyes swallowed her up. Just as they had the night they made love. 'Don't be so afraid.'

'I'm not afraid.'

His smile told her she wasn't kidding anyone.

So she added, 'It's just that this is the craziest idea ever. We don't know each other.'

'We'll get to know one another. You don't have to do everything in life by the book.' He lowered his head closer to her and whispered, 'We can make this work, trust me.'

Her heart dipped and then soared in her chest.

He spoke with such strength, determination, even kindness, she forgot every reason why this could never work and said with a gulp, 'Can we?'

His hand reached out and for a moment rested just above her hip. She stopped breathing. She fought the urge to move in closer. Longing to feel his arms wrapped around her, his body pushed against hers.

His gaze moved to her tummy and then back up to hers.

He lowered his head, his lips not far away from hers.

She fell into the green burning depths of his eyes.

His breath whispered across her lips.

She swayed closer.

His eyes burnt even brighter. And then his lips brushed against her cheek until he reached her ear. In a low voice he whispered, 'We'll make this work.' His hand cupped her hip even more. 'I'll make sure it does.'

And then he was moving to the door. 'Our appointment is at nine-thirty tomorrow. I will collect you at nine-fifteen.'

Dazed, she stared after him.

A gut-wrenching thought hit her.

Had she just witnessed a master manipulator at work?

She followed him to the front door, resolute that she was going to say no to everything he was proposing. There was no way she was agreeing to marrying this expert schemer...player... heartbreaker.

But before she could speak he turned and, with a quiet, intent dignity, he said, 'I will be the best father and husband that I can. I'll change my way of working, my socialising. I will be faithful to *all* of my marriage vows.' He paused and his hand moved close to where her belly lay beneath her sweater top, his fingers tipping against the navy cotton. 'Why wouldn't I, when I have something so special waiting for me at home?'

CHAPTER THREE

Wednesday 20th April, 10:45 p.m.

This is my private number. Contact me any time you need me.

LATER THAT EVENING Lucien pressed 'send' on his text and went back to the never-ending stream of emails awaiting his attention. His stomach growled. He needed food. He had missed the gala dinner he had been scheduled to attend tonight in Palais Brongniart in favour of returning to London.

Knowing that decisive action was needed.

Knowing that he had to cut off any ideas Charlotte had of excluding him from their lives before that idea became entrenched.

And if that took marrying her, so be it.

He was doing the right thing.

He had a duty to his unborn child.

Unlike his own parents, he *would* be a responsible parent.

But that did not stop the whispers of doubts that were creeping into his bloodstream. Could he make this work? Would he mess up as a father, as a husband? He had failed as a husband once before. Would he do so again?

His phone pinged and the screen glowed in the low light of his home office. He grabbed it impatiently, annoyed to admit to himself that he had been waiting for her response.

I understand why you want to be part of my child's life. But why do you want us to marry? C

After his first marriage had failed he had sworn never to marry again. Hurt and angry at the endless arguments, sick in his heart at his own weaknesses that led to the marriage imploding. Sick at the knowledge that he was no better than his own spineless father. He had been repulsed the day he had found his father in the act of betraying his mother with another woman.

But not repulsed enough to fight the weak nature he had obviously inherited from him. For Lucien had gone on to betray his first wife, Gabrielle. A betrayal driven by anger and jealousy and hurt and pain. He had found Gabrielle seminaked in the arms of another man and in pathetic revenge had gone out and slept with another woman. Frantic to ease the panic and loneliness that had threatened to crush him, knowing that there was no one in this world he could trust.

But now an unexpected need to protect his own

was hammering through him and it pushed even his fears of marriage, of how it would expose the coward at the heart of him, to the side. He stabbed out his response.

I don't want our child to have any doubt about how much he's wanted, or about our commitment to raising him together. This is a public commitment to our baby.

After ten minutes of waiting for a response, he gave in to his hunger and was cooking fresh spinach and ricotta ravioli he had found in his fridge when her response finally came.

It might be a girl. C

Puzzled, he checked back on his previous text and saw he had unwittingly referred to the baby as a boy.

He popped a white grape from a bunch he had also taken from the fridge into his mouth. And then crunched down on another. And another. The sweet but sharp juice easing the dryness in his throat. His heart did a funny little shiver. He was going to be the father of a boy. How he knew he had no idea. But he knew. The knot of tension eating into his neck all day tightened even more.

He texted back.

It's a boy.

He was plating his pasta when his phone lit up again.

Do you really want to do this? I know you are impulsive in work, in the decisions you take, but this is about a baby, not a business deal you can walk away from if it doesn't work out. C.

He dropped the bottle of olive oil he was holding onto the smooth concrete of the kitchen counter. He could still back out of this. See the baby at weekends. And at other agreed times.

He wouldn't have the same opportunity to mess up his son's life when he wasn't a constant presence in his life.

He wouldn't have the constant fear of his marriage descending into a toxic mess.

He wouldn't have to deal with the fire that burned between him and Charlotte whenever they were in the same room. A fire that could easily derail their plans to raise their child together if expectations and emotions became confused.

But he owed it to his son to make him feel the most wanted child in this world. And he would do anything to ensure that his son *never* doubted his father's love.

He punched in his response.

I will never walk away from my son.

He ate his pasta in silence. What was Charlotte thinking? Was she getting cold feet? He typed in another text.

Will collect you at nine-fifteen tomorrow. I'm travelling to Rome after the register office and then on to Asia and the US but I'll keep in contact.

Again silence. He tossed his now empty plate into the dishwasher and grabbed his phone.

I will curtail my travel when the baby is born.

Sitting on her sofa in her pyjamas, Charlotte laid her hand on her stomach. Was it slightly more rounded than usual?

Was there really a life growing inside there?

She sighed in confusion at the conflicting thoughts looping through her brain: why would she want to lose her independence?

But then why would she choose to face being a parent on her own?

Why would she choose to marry a maverick heartbreaker?

But then why would she deny her child the right to have her father in her life on a daily basis?

And what of her career? She would struggle to

get a job as challenging and rewarding and with so much potential for progression outside London.

But would Lucien be a feckless father?

Or could he love his child as much as her own father loved her?

A large lump swelled in her throat. She adored her father, his old-fashioned gentlemanly ways, his sense of fairness, his love for her mum, his dry sense of humour. The way his eyes lit up whenever he saw her.

But against all of this constant jabber and these conflicting thoughts, one solid feeling pumped in her heart.

She had to do everything to protect her child's future.

Which had to include taking steps now to protect her baby should anything ever happen to her. She inhaled a deep breath and with trembling fingers managed to type.

The only reason I'm agreeing to this marriage is so that my baby has a hands-on, loving and attentive father in her life. If you aren't those things, if work and your social life interferes, we are walking away. C

After pressing 'send' she switched off the phone and threw it into the far corner of the couch. Instead of resigning tomorrow she would be registering to marry her CEO. She stood and walked towards her bedroom. Praying she knew what she was doing.

Thursday 21st April, 11:10 p.m.

Why aren't you answering my calls?

Sorry. Was busy. Had to work late to catch up after our appointment at the registrar's office this morning. What do you want? C

To check how you are.

I'm fine. Thanks. Night. C

Friday 22nd April, 4:54 p.m.

Still busy, I take it? Or is it just my calls you aren't taking?

I'm at work. Personal calls aren't allowed. C

Funny. Ring me. I want to speak to you about the Poole project. It's almost midnight here in Singapore so call within the next half-hour.

Sorry can't. In a meeting. C

How are you?

Great. Got to go. C

Saturday 23rd April, 12:30 p.m.

Just arrived into Tokyo. What are your plans for the weekend?

Going to visit my parents. Will tell them about baby and our wedding. C

How will they react?

I don't know. C

Wait for me to return to London. I'll be back on 30th.

Why? C

I want to support you. And I'm guessing they'll want to meet me.

I need to do this by myself. C

Why?

It's easier to pretend to be in love with you when you're not standing in the same room. C

Tuesday 26th April, 10:30 p.m.

How's Tokyo? C

In Las Vegas now.

Mixing with lots of pretty showgirls? C

I'm on a construction site.

I told my mum and dad. They're thrilled about the baby. Shocked but happy about the wedding. C

Good.

Wednesday 27th April, 9:14 p.m.

Won your fortune in Las Vegas yet? C

Moved on to New York last night.

Lucky you. Love New York. C

How are you?

I'm okay. Morning sickness still here. C

'You didn't tell me.

It's not important—most women suffer when pregnant. C

Take time off work. You should have told me.

You didn't tell me that you had been married before. C

You're annoyed?

I'd have preferred not to have found out when we were in the register office. C

It was a long time ago. Have you seen a doctor about your sickness?

Yes. She assured me it's completely normal. C

You have to take care of yourself and the baby.

We haven't spoken about telling people at work yet. C

I have a plan that I'll discuss with you when I'm back in London on Saturday. Come to my house for dinner.

There's a new restaurant in Soho I've been wanting to try. Let's meet there. I'll book and send you the details. We also need to talk about a pre-nuptial agreement. I don't want anything from you. C

We'll have more privacy to talk in my house.

Somebody at the door. Have to go. C

Charlotte grimaced at the gingernut biscuit crumbs that had landed on her desk. *And in her keyboard!* Just—*yuck.*

Now she remembered why she had quickly given up eating at her desk as a young intern.

She twisted the keyboard upside down and shook vigorously. A woman in an online pregnancy forum swore that ginger biscuits kept her nausea at bay.

Charlotte wasn't convinced but at least the biscuits might give her a temporary sugar high to beat the tiredness that sat heavy in her bones.

She wasn't sleeping well.

In a matter of days she had gone from avoiding calls and texts from Lucien to being addicted to checking her phone to see if he had left a message.

In the first few days when he had gone, she had been unable to handle talking to him. Too overwhelmed with how her life had changed. And shocked to know that he had been married before. It shouldn't have been a surprise, but it left her feeling more vulnerable. It brought home how little she knew him.

She had needed space and time away from him. Away from how she seemed to lose her ability to think logically when in his presence, even if that was an electronic one. So she hadn't answered his calls and kept her texts brief, immersing herself instead in finalising the new mentoring programme she was introducing into the department for their new interns.

But when he had stopped texting over the weekend, she realised how much she missed hearing from him, missed knowing that he was thinking about her, even if it was only because she was carrying his child.

But last night when he had suggested that they meet at his house on Saturday to talk it had hit home just how difficult it would be to live under the same roof as him, especially in a house full of memories and reminders of their night together.

Was she doing the right thing?

A large crumb stubbornly refused to budge from under the space bar. She shook the keyboard hard and it dropped down to her desk.

Only when she had settled the keyboard back onto the desk did she realise that the entire office was staring at her. Even Simon, in the midst of a phone call, was staring out at her from his office window with his mouth open.

And then she realised that all of the eyes were trailing from her to a point behind her shoulder.

She turned slowly in her swivel chair.

Standing there, green eyes fixed on her, almost devouring her, wearing a smile that pinged her heart right out of her chest, a huge hand-tied bunch of tulips in his arms and, most worrying of all, a robin-egg-blue jewellery box in his hand, was Lucien.

Her throat sealed over. But aware of all of her colleagues staring at her, she managed to garble out, 'You're back early.' Two days early to be precise.

That incredible smile broadened. Who was this imposter? Lucien Duval scowled. He didn't smile.

He handed her the white and pink tipped tulips.

She accepted them, gave her flabbergasted colleagues who worked behind her a faint smile and said in a rush, 'Maybe we should go and talk somewhere more private.'

But instead, he dropped down to one knee and said, 'I know we're only dating a short while but you have become the centre of my world, especially now that you're to be the mother of my child.'

There was a collective gasp from the audience surrounding them, which did absolutely nothing to knock Lucien off course.

Opening the blue box, he lifted a much too

beautiful and elegant three-diamond and platinum ring towards her. 'Charlotte, *veux-tu m'épouser*? Will you marry me?'

She wanted to scream *no*. She wanted to shout at him for doing this. For asking her in such a low, sensual, sexy voice that she couldn't stop her legs from jingling against the central frame of her chair. For mortifying her like this. For piercing her heart with those intense green eyes.

But she had no option but to nod her acceptance, hoping that her colleagues thought that her hand was clasped to her mouth in shocked happiness rather than horror.

Wolf whistles, applause and cheers sounded in the room.

Lucien stood and, taking the ring from the box, placed it on her finger.

She tried to yank her hand away but he only tightened his grip more firmly and pulled her up to stand before him.

'Kiss, kiss, kiss.'

Charlotte looked beseechingly towards the intern corner, willing them to stop their chant. But her appeal only egged on the duo of mischievous male interns who shouted even louder for them to kiss, their female counterparts openly ogling Lucien close to swooning at any moment.

With a quick tug he pulled her towards him, an

amused glint in those sinful green eyes the last thing she saw before his lips landed on hers.

It was a soft kiss.

Teasing, torturous, tantalising.

She stumbled closer into him, her hand reaching out to balance herself.

The hard thump of his heart beat against her palm beneath his lightweight grey suit jacket.

For a moment she became lost to the weight of his hand on her waist, the hardness of his chest, the scent of a freshly showered man.

When he pulled away, her already burning cheeks fired even hotter with the crazy compulsion to have their kiss continue.

She stumbled back from him.

Tried to smile as her colleagues clapped once again.

She plastered a rictus smile on lips that felt stupidly swollen for what was a relatively chaste kiss. On tippy toes she reached up to his ear, her colleagues probably thinking she was whispering a sweet nothing to him when in fact she snarled, 'We need to talk. *Now.*'

On the top floor, inside his office, Charlotte shut the door and leaned against it with an infuriated sigh. 'Do you care to explain what on earth the past ten minutes has been about?'

'Assertive public relations.'

'Meaning?'

'The key to any public relations is to get in there first with how you want to present a story. My proposing to you publicly has taken away the power of any speculation as to why we're marrying. Now that it's out in the open it will only be office gossip for ten minutes max rather than weeks of water-cooler gossip.'

'I didn't think you cared.'

'I want my staff focused on work not their CEO's relationship with another employee. Also, you now have a ring and a story to tell your parents, if you're still determined to pretend to them that we're in love.'

Charlotte gritted her teeth. She was so annoyed on so many different levels she didn't know where to start. Lucien Duval needed to be taken down a peg or two. And he had to learn that this was a relationship of equals, which included not always being the one with the upper hand. A hard lesson to learn for a CEO who liked to always have things his way.

She smiled at him sweetly.

He looked at her suspiciously.

She dropped her head to the side and shrugged innocently. 'That's okay. I already told my parents that I took you to Paris and proposed to you there.'

His familiar scowl reappeared with a vengeance. 'Well, you can *un*-tell them.'

'Nope. Can't do. My mum, though shocked at first, was actually chuffed that I took matters into my own hands. I told my parents that on balance I thought you'd make an ideal father, I'm guessing you're good at sport so you'll be handy on sports day, you speak native French so the baby will be bilingual and I'm hoping you'll be handy around the house.' She gave him an unapologetic smile. 'Anyway I'm sticking by my story…especially after the stunt you just pulled.'

He considered her for a moment, dark brows pinched, shrugged off his jacket and placed it on his desk and advanced towards her, a wicked gleam now shining brightly in his eyes. 'You didn't object to our kiss.'

He was doing it again.

Invading her personal space, his big body making her feel tiny, making her body swim with want.

She stared at the crisp brightness of his white shirt and tried to ignore the pull of his clean soapy scent. The image of him in his shower…

She had to remember that he was a player. That she couldn't trust him. If her *'regular guy'* ex could break her heart, imagine what devastation an astute alpha charmer could inflict.

Memories of her shattered heart, the hollowing-out loneliness of being heartbroken coupled with her depression, shot steel back into her spine. She placed her hand on the door handle and said icily, 'I'm good at faking my responses.'

His eyes duelled with hers. She tried not to blink. Not to look away. The gleam in his eye shifted from wicked to evil. 'You enjoyed it and you know it.'

She pressed the door handle down. 'Not enough for it to happen again.'

'That sounds like a challenge.'

What was she doing? Antagonising, provoking, challenging a man who thrived on confronting obstacles. It was like poking a sleeping grizzly bear with a stick. She pushed down on the door handle even more, ready to make a quick exit once she had said her piece. 'Well, it's just as well then that we both know that our marriage is nothing more than a front for raising our child. I'm sure I can rely on you not to jeopardise our child's happiness by confusing the reasons why we're together.'

His brows slammed together.

And then as though he couldn't help himself, that risk-taking maverick at the heart of him shining through, he placed his foot against the base of the door, preventing her exit, and said with a glint in his eye, 'Deny away, Charlotte. There's nothing I like more in life than to prove others wrong.'

CHAPTER FOUR

SHE HAD TO be kidding.

The following month, Lucien watched Charlotte emerge from a classic silver Bentley, festooned with white ribbon, to the applause of the 'small' wedding party.

Dressed in a knee-length, full-skirted white bridal dress, Charlotte accepted her father's outstretched hand—well, he was guessing it was her father—and cuddled into his side, a wide smile on her mouth. Her father, tall and upright, handsome with slicked-back steel-grey hair, slowly leaned down and kissed her forehead.

Dieu! The Verbal Assassin had turned into a blushing bride.

The wedding party began to make their way up the tree-lined cobbled forecourt. Charlotte said something to her father and broke away, approaching him on her own, her father stopping to chat to a woman wearing a flying-saucer-sized hat.

He smiled at her, the ever dutiful groom, temporarily forgetting all of his grievances as he was sucked into this pantomime, for a moment almost believing that the gorgeous woman smiling and blushing shyly at him was his willing and loving bride.

He pulled himself together, his frustration spiking dangerously, and when she was close enough he growled, 'The registrar is running late. We have to wait outside here until they are ready.'

Just then a photographer arrived and in a stage whisper said, 'Don't mind me, I'll just snap away. Try to be as natural as you can be.'

Lucien reined in the urge to grab his camera and toss it in the nearest bush and instead pointed the photographer in the direction of his friend Rakesh. 'Take some photos of him and the other witness.' He paused and waited while Charlotte directed him towards her friend Tameka.

When the photographer had scuttled away he said, 'I thought this was going to be a simple ceremony. It makes a royal wedding look tame.'

She glanced at the pedestals of pink, lilac and white flowers lining the pathway, the pink and silver balloons tied to the trunks of the trees flapping in the warm May air and gave a guilty smile. 'My mum got a little carried away.'

'You don't say. I was half expecting you to arrive in a horse and carriage. Why didn't you warn me?'

She smiled at him sweetly but her eyes damned him. 'If I'd seen you during the past two weeks maybe I would have.'

A thread of guilt poked his gut and, not wanting to think about it, he answered with a shrug, 'I had to be in Asia for negotiations.'

'So you said.'

Her hair was coiled into a low bun to the side of her head, a large white silk flower threaded just above her right ear. The picture-perfect bride. A wave of frustration and panic swirled in his chest. This was supposed to be a quick, no-nonsense ceremony. A business deal. Had Charlotte already confused the nature of their agreement? 'Why didn't you stop your mother? Surely you don't want all of this fuss too?'

She adjusted the satin bodice of her dress. 'Obviously not, but as my mum had hoped I'd get married in my village church with the entire village in attendance, I wasn't going to deny her a few flowers and balloons, was I?'

He tried not to stare at her, to fully acknowledge to himself just how stunningly pretty she looked.

He flexed his jaw and nodded towards the noisy, laughing crowd behind them, mostly made up of men who looked like retired army officers and their stalwarts-of-the-community wives. Good people who would be horrified at the truth of their marriage. 'Flowers and balloons I could handle, but did they have to invite such a large crowd?'

She nodded and scowled towards where Rakesh was blatantly chatting up Tameka, the photographer snapping Rakesh's rakish smile and Tameka's blush. 'Twenty-four people is hardly a crowd. There's over two hundred people in the village. So count yourself lucky. Just because you decided to only invite a fellow playboy to the wedding didn't mean that I was going to restrict the number of guests my parents wanted to invite. It's a moment of celebration for them, even if it's closer to being a funeral for you.' She regarded him with an evil smile playing on her lips. 'I'm guessing it would have been too humiliating to have more than one witness to the death of your womanising days.'

Dieu, she had a special gift for needling him.

He had only invited one guest because this was no more than an agreement to raise their child together. The last thing he had wanted was a circus around what should be a simple ceremony.

He ignored the voice that came from deep within him, pointing out that in truth he had no one else close enough to him to invite.

With irritation gnawing his insides, he leaned down towards her.

For a moment he became disorientated. She smelt different. Gone was the smell of starched cotton and paperwork. Now she smelt of light and sunshine.

Who was he marrying?

The ice-cool lawyer of work or the vulnerable, gentle woman he had made love to in his bed?

He drew back.

Familiar unimpressed sea-green eyes held his gaze.

This woman, the tough, cynical lawyer, he could handle.

Reassured, he gave her a slow smile and a husky whisper. 'Trust me, I'm looking forward to being a one-woman man.'

She dropped her head to the side. 'Best of luck in finding her. Anyway, I guess I should introduce you to my parents. Or do you have a sudden need to get away again? Any crisis in the New York office that only Super Lucien can sort out?'

He cupped her cheek and stroked her skin with his thumb. Lifted her chin, forcing her to meet his gaze. 'I've already told you, you're the only woman in my life from now on. Get used to that fact.'

Something shifted in her expression. She bit her lip and said softly,, 'You can still call this off. It's not too late.'

Her gaze was nervous, almost pleading. Doubt swirled in his chest. Should he call it off? Could he be a good husband to this woman? But then his eyes drifted down to the waistband of her dress, her gently rounded belly catching slightly on the material.

A reminder of why they had to go through with this.

He caught her by the elbow and twisted her

around slowly towards the wedding guests, shards of sunshine breaking through the leafy trees overhead, dancing on the cobbled path. 'And cause a scandal in the village? I don't think so.'

As they approached the guests Charlotte's father and a flustered-looking woman in her mid-seventies broke away from the other guests to meet them.

'Mum, Dad, this is Lucien.'

From her dad he received a firm handshake and an unflinching military stare. Her mum rushed forward and yanked him down into a mama-bear-type hug. For a moment he thought he had whiplash.

Disconcerted, he cleared his throat and moved back two steps. 'Monsieur and Madame Aldridge, my apologies for cancelling our lunch last Sunday.'

A bundle of feathers and what looked like painted pink straw in Charlotte's mum's short grey hair quivered when she answered. 'Oh, call us by our first names, Robert and Carol, and don't worry about last weekend. Lottie explained how you decided to go on a weekend course called How to be a Good Husband—what will they think of next? But such a good idea. I must say between your weekend course and accepting Lottie's proposal, you really are one of these *New Men* I read about in the newspapers.'

Charlotte patted him on the arm. 'Oh, Lucien

really is a *New Man*, ready to embrace his softer side. I already see a change in how he's communicating with me. And he's so in tune with my needs. Aren't you, darling?'

He gritted his teeth and addressed her mother, 'Lottie?'

Taken aback, her mum gestured towards Charlotte. 'Lottie, of course, it's our pet name for Charlotte—didn't she ever tell you that?'

Her father and mother moved closer to one another and stared at him dubiously. He placed an arm around Charlotte's shoulders and tucked her against his chest. '*Dieu!* You have to forgive me… I'm a little jet-lagged right now. I've got into the habit of calling Charlotte *ma minette*: my pussy-cat.'

Charlotte swung her hand up to rest beneath his jacket and gave a loud chuckle. Her fingertips dug into his side. 'I've told you, darling, just call me Charlotte. Lottie and *ma minette* don't suit me.'

He forced himself to smile down at her, his skin stinging.

Her father cleared his throat and said sombrely, 'Lottie said that your parents are unable to make the wedding. It's a shame they couldn't be here.'

Fed up of all the lies and how Charlotte kept playing games with him, he gave an extravagant shrug. 'Not really. We haven't spoken in almost twenty years. We don't get on.'

For a moment alarm bells flashed in both of her parents' eyes. And rather satisfyingly, Charlotte looked up at him as if she was ready to take him apart.

Her mum was the first to break the tense silence. With a loud sigh she said, 'Oh, well…never mind. You'll be part of our family now.'

Charlotte's body stiffened beneath his hold. 'Mum, please.'

He dropped his arm and stepped away.

Her mother continued, looking at him with earnest ecstasy, 'We can't tell you, Lucien, how thrilled we are about the baby.'

Charlotte's frown dropped and she looked at her mum with a wistful indulgent smile.

Her father interjected by stepping forward. 'We hope that you're both very happy together. Lottie means the world to us, when—'

Charlotte interrupted her father in a low pleading voice, 'Dad, please.'

For a moment all three shared looks that spoke of family bonds, of family secrets. Bonds and secrets that excluded him. A wave of loneliness caught him unawares. Had he ever been as close to anyone in his life where a single look could communicate so much?

His voice unsteady, Charlotte's father continued, 'We hope more than anything that you have a long and happy life together. Be kind and patient with one another.'

Charlotte hugged her dad and then her mum, who was busy wiping away tears.

Lucien fisted his hands against the guilt and inadequacy that exploded inside him. He already had a failed marriage, parents who were the antithesis of role models when it came to parenting. He should end this charade. Her parents should know the truth: that he couldn't give their daughter all of the things they wanted for her—he was not capable of being the husband they expected. He wasn't even certain he was capable of being the father their grandson deserved.

Was Charlotte right? Should they call this off?

He muttered something in agreement and was relieved when Charlotte suggested that she introduce him to her friends.

When they were out of earshot he said furiously, 'We need to tell them the truth.'

Charlotte came to a stop and, with a pained smile on her lips, muttered through clenched teeth, 'If you hurt my parents I will never forgive you.'

With that she walked away.

His soon-to-be infuriating wife.

Could he, should he go through with this? His life was going to be turned upside down. A new baby, a wife, in-laws. How on earth was he going to focus on work and the daily crises needing his attention? How on earth was he going to handle the suffocating bonds of family, the fear of messing up his marriage, the fear of failing his son?

If Charlotte had ever allowed herself to stop and think about what her perfect wedding ceremony would look like, this would probably be it. A small intimate venue in a historic house, her parents present, spring sunshine flooding into the room from a large bow window, a garden outside filled with vibrant-coloured gladioli swaying in the light breeze and the promise of another long energetic and exciting summer in London. A violin soloist playing. And at her side a man who made her heart leap every time she saw him. A man who took her normal physical reserve and tore it into strips just by being him, all six-foot-two, muscular, hard, sneering him. A tough-skinned business maverick who got what he wanted in life through brutal persuasion and a dangerous intelligence. A player. A heartbreaker.

The registrar invited them to stand to say their vows.

She stood and clasped her trembling hands.

And looked into the clear green eyes of the man she was about to marry.

They had emailed each other back and forth

various versions of their vows for the past week, until they had found a version they were both comfortable with.

His attention focused solely on her, Lucien repeated after the registrar, 'I, Lucien Duval, take you, Charlotte Aldridge, as my wife. I promise to create and protect a family and home that's full of love, understanding, respect and honour.'

Lucien paused and swallowed hard.

The lines around his eyes tightened.

Her stomach somersaulted, sadness, tenderness dragged in her chest.

Lucien Duval, street-savvy maverick CEO, looked lost.

Without thinking she reached out to him.

He took her hand in his. For the longest moment he held her gaze, doubt in his eyes.

Was he about to back out?

She closed her eyes.

Her heart sank down into her chest.

Heavy with...what? Was it disappointment that was weighing it down so fiercely?

His fingers gripped hers and pulled her ever so slightly closer to him.

She opened her eyes to his intense stare.

And for that moment they were the only people in the room.

It would be so easy to fall in love with him.

Her heart went into overdrive. She mustn't. But it would be so easy.

In a low sombre voice, his eyes not wavering from hers, Lucien continued with his vows. 'I promise to be always open and honest. And, whatever may come, promise to provide you with comfort and support through life's joy and sorrow.'

It was her turn.

But her mouth wouldn't co-operate.

I'm about to marry this man who takes my breath away. This totally unsuitable man. I've lost my mind.

She smiled guiltily to the registrar, who had whispered her name a number of times. Nodded to say that she was okay.

Looked back at Lucien.

Her pulse pounded even harder.

Could she go through with this?

Lucien stepped in towards her. And held her hand with both of his. As though offering her his strength. He regarded her with a dignity that tightened her chest.

She took a deep breath and repeated her vows. 'I, Charlotte Aldridge, take you, Lucien Duval, as my husband. I promise to create and protect a family and home that's full of love, understanding, respect and honour.'

She paused and fought the tears that sprang up

in her eyes, saying the words aloud, in front of friends and family, reminding her of why they were marrying. To create a family. This was all about their baby.

Handing Lucien their marriage certificate, the registrar invited them to stand. With a smile she introduced them to their guests as man and wife. And after the applause died down, she invited them to kiss.

Her stomach headed south.

Lucien gave her that *Well, what are we going to do now?* smile, which had proved her undoing that night they'd slept together. Beguiling, playful, safe, inviting.

His hand reached up and his thumb slowly ran along her jawline.

As though treasuring what was before him.

His green eyes didn't hold their usual shrewdness. Instead he considered her almost tenderly… sweetly.

His fingers ran down the side of her neck.

Her back arched.

The room was in silence. Without looking she knew their guests were staring at them, breaths held, waiting for their kiss.

He angled his head. His eyes darkened. The flattering, intoxicating, hard-to-resist gaze of a

man who was looking at something he wanted.
A lot.

She moved a little closer. Moved up onto her
tippy toes.

He gave a small smile, pulled her towards him
and kissed her gently. His lips teasing hers.

In an instant she was melting against him,
drugged by the taste of his mouth, his clean leathery scent, the pull of his big body.

She felt his hand rest on her tummy. Lightly,
protectively, possessively.

A silent reminder of why they were standing
here as husband and wife, kissing.

The pretence of a relationship for the sake of
their child.

Half an hour later, the Bentley slowly passed the
Elephant and Castle, the early Friday rush hour
slowing their journey northwards to their reception venue.

Beside her, Lucien was still pulling grains of
rice from his hair and suit pocket.

Every now and then their driver would gaze at
them in his rear-view mirror, obviously puzzled at
the tense silence between the newlyweds.

She ran her hands down over the satin of her
dress. Despite everything this dress represented—
a sham marriage, the loss of her independence,
having to pretend she wasn't magnetised to her

groom—she loved its simple elegance. Though it had got a little too tight in the past week—the changes in her body were becoming more pronounced with each passing day—she had actually been pleased when she had looked at her reflection in the mirror in her bedroom earlier. But now she just felt deflated.

The need to end the awful and telling silence between them had her say, 'Well, I guess we must hold the record for the shortest ever wedding photoshoot.'

'The photographer had ten minutes—how long more did he need?'

'The poor man looked crushed when you refused to stand in for more photos. And there I was hoping for a few shots of us paddling in the fountain in the park next door—I thought it would look cute on—' she paused and forced herself to say '—our mantelpiece.' Was she really going to live with Lucien Duval? Her CEO. The playboy serial dater. Live with him…as his wife. Would this ever feel normal and not half fantasy, half nightmare?

Lucien's only response was a disbelieving exhalation before he began to flick through his phone.

Irritated, she said, 'We don't have to go to the reception if you don't want to.'

He threw her a quick glance, but there was a hint of amusement lurking there. 'And miss whatever wonderful surprises your mother has organised? I don't think so.'

Stupidly buoyed up by this change in his humour, she said with a wry teasing smile, 'It's nothing really special—just a champagne reception, a five-course meal with an accompanying jazz band in Claridge's.'

He threw his eyes to heaven and dropped his phone down onto the seat between them. He turned and stared at her for a moment, the humour in his eyes slowly fading. 'Why is this wedding so important to your parents?'

After Dan's and Angie's betrayal, she had boxed away any thoughts and dreams she had of boyfriends, a fiancé, a husband. Too hurt and scared to even contemplate those things any more.

But despite her terrible relationship history, propelled by a low-lying loneliness, over the past few years she had occasionally scurried out of her comfortable world of work and gym classes to date. And after a few skirmishes she would quickly retreat, hating the games involved, the second guessing, the vulnerability of putting yourself and your heart on the line. The need to mind and protect herself easily defeating the need for intimacy and closeness.

Now, to answer his question she gestured to her dress with a wry grimace. 'I've always said I wanted to focus on my career and that relationships weren't important to me, so they never expected to see me dressed in a meringue. They weren't the only ones.' Her mocking tone died in her mouth and she cleared her throat, her heart pounding, not sure why she felt so compelled to share with him what was scaring her so much. 'My dad isn't well—he has heart problems.'

He considered her for much too long, those green eyes eating her up, the usual hardness in his expression softening. 'I'm sorry to hear that.'

Her heart dropped into her stomach and bounced back at double its normal speed. He had spoken in a low, kind voice. The voice he had whispered to her with, that night they had spent together. She bit the inside of her lip, trying to stop the thickness in her throat from building any more.

He twisted further in his seat, laid a hand on the seat between them, his fingertips almost touching the satin of her skirt. 'You worry about them?'

Without thinking she answered, 'Almost as much as they worry about me.'

She had argued with her mum and dad the weekend she had told them about the baby and her engagement, over whether she should tell Lucien about her depression. They insisted that she should. But she had refused to even discuss the issue with them.

Talking about her depression still felt as if she

had to rip her soul out and expose it for the whole world to see.

What good could come from burdening Lucien with her past health history anyway?

It *was* in the past.

Aware that Lucien was waiting for her to explain what she meant about her parents worrying about her, she opted to focus the conversation on him instead. 'Why don't you talk to your parents?'

The mellow, empathic Lucien disappeared in a long slow blink of his dark eyelashes to be replaced by the familiar street-fighter blank stare. 'I hit my dad when I found him in bed with another woman. Two years later I hit my mum's new boyfriend even harder.'

She gasped at the bluntness of his answer. The lack of emotion in his voice. She muttered, 'Why?' while wincing inside at the brief disappointment that flickered on his features at her shocked response.

In a bored tone he said, 'I don't think this is a subject matter for a wedding day, even a convenience one like ours.'

They were now driving through Green Park via Constitution Hill, past tourists heading to and from Buckingham Palace, past commuters rushing home for the weekend. Hearing the bitterness in his voice, his dismissal of their wedding day, had her turn to him and ask a question that she knew was going to lead to a whole series of questions she had to ask, questions that were starting to drive her insane.

She tried to keep her voice neutral, the voice of a colleague passing time on a shared journey. 'How old were you when you married the first time round?'

He considered her for a moment, a chess master sizing up his opposition. 'Eighteen.'

'And your wife?'

He now seemed intrigued as to where she was going with this. 'Eighteen too.' He rose an eyebrow as though to say, *Well, what's coming next?*

Inside logic was screaming at her not to ask. But she couldn't stop herself. How could she compete with an eighteen-year-old? No wonder he hadn't said one thing about how she looked today. Couldn't he at least have said she looked *nice*? That innocuous word that covered general okayishness and all sorts of wardrobe malfunctions?

'Was she beautiful?'

He looked at her in exasperation. But then turned and stared out at the hotels on Park Lane. 'I don't remember.'

She gave a tight laugh full of mocking derision. Derision for her own vain stupidity and her own lack of self-esteem, driven by the prowling image of herself, thin and grey and exhausted, facing a too-loved-up-to-hide-the-evidence Dan and Angie that had her wanting, needing Lucien to find her attractive on their wedding day, even if it was all a charade. 'And you said you don't like to lie.'

He twisted back to her. Frustration burned in his eyes. 'Yes, she was pretty…but not as beautiful as you look today.' He inhaled, ran a hand down over his face. He settled now softer, sad even, eyes on her and in a quiet voice he added, 'Please…don't make this any harder than it has to be. There's too much at stake.'

Something cracked inside her heart. She had to work against the tightness in her throat before she managed to say, 'You're right. Sorry.'

His hand gently landed on hers, his fingers splayed across hers. Followed by a look full of resigned regret but also a hint of warmth and understanding.

His fingers curled around her hand and he looked back out into the streets of London.

He held her hand all the way to Claridge's.

And for the first time she fully realised that for better or worse they were now a couple, a team, a husband and wife. Not in the conventional sense, of course, they hadn't got traditional romantic love, but they did have something just as important bonding them together for ever: a love for their child.

CHAPTER FIVE

FOUR HOURS LATER, Lucien led Charlotte into the kitchen of his Mayfair home.

Now her home too, of course.

His wife.

The mother-to-be of his child.

Dieu! Would he ever get used to all of this?

He swung open the folding doors that ran the length of the back kitchen wall, a brilliant sunset just about to drop below the coach house to the rear of the garden.

It was still warm enough to sit outside so he gestured to the garden furniture out on the terrace. 'You must be tired. Take a seat and I'll get you a drink.'

Her gaze trailed out into the garden and paused for the briefest moment on the garden wall in the near right corner. To the spot where their child had been conceived in a moment of intoxicating, passionate madness.

She gave him a tight smile. 'Tea would be nice. Do you have any decaf?'

He nodded and twisted away. Hoping that with time both of their memories would fade of that night. Because right now, those memories were torturing him with unleashed desire.

He jerked on the water tap, filled the kettle and placed it on the hob. And then snapped open his coffee machine. Until he remembered.

He switched it off. And yanked open his fridge and took out a bottle of sparkling water.

Charlotte considered the bottle and then him. 'You can have a coffee if you want. I'm able to tolerate the smell now.'

'It's fine.'

She shrugged, and sat down on a stool at the far side of the breakfast counter, a hand running along the poured concrete countertop surface. 'Or have something stronger if you'd like. You haven't drunk all day. Just because I can't drink alcohol, doesn't mean you aren't able to.'

In her white princess dress, her hair coiled to the side of her head, she looked like the ballerina figure that used to twirl around and around when he opened his mother's jewellery box.

Would he ever manage to look at her without it doing something peculiar to his heart, without being possessed with a burning need to reach out and touch her?

Dieu!

He was worn out from spending the day trying not to notice her.

Their first dance on the small dance floor in the private dining room where their reception had been held had been an uncomfortable blend of awkwardness and a strange intimacy, the vivid memories of their night together alive and intense as he held her slight frame in his arms, and the bond of creating a child tying them together more powerfully than if they had known each other for years.

'I don't drink alcohol.'

'Really?'

He rested against the kitchen countertop opposite her and folded his arms. 'Not what you expected from a serial dater who enjoys breaking women's hearts?'

She shrugged with a hint of guilty admission at his reminder of her previous accusation and said, 'I have to admit that I had assumed drinking went along with your lifestyle.'

Once upon a time it had. In his late teens he had used alcohol to numb the gnawing emptiness inside him, but it had only made the emptiness more overwhelming and had fuelled a self-destructive anger that had led him to ending his marriage through the weakest, most cowardly, most pathetic act possible.

'We have a lot to find out about each other,' he said, turning away to make her tea, adding with his back to her, 'I hate not being in control.'

'Should I be worried—you're not a control freak, are you?'

Her voice was teasing.

He turned and raised an eyebrow. 'Hardly. I put

up with the extravaganza that was our supposedly simple wedding ceremony today, didn't I?'

She grimaced and asked, 'Was today really that horrible for you?'

Despite himself he admitted the truth. 'All things considered, it was a nice day. Your mum did a good job.'

She smiled and lifted the cup he had placed before her. 'Thanks for playing along today, for keeping up the story...' she cleared her throat, and stared down at her cup '...that we're in love... It means a lot to me. I would hate to upset my parents. As you probably could tell, they're very protective of me.'

They looked at each other in silence for a few seconds too long, awkwardness, tension, the enormity of what they were doing hanging between them once again.

He forced himself to speak. 'Why so?'

Her eyes shifted away from him, she shrugged, moved in her seat, adjusting her gown beneath her. 'My parents were relatively old when I arrived. They had been told they couldn't have children so I was a surprise...a much-wanted surprise. They were pretty strict and old-fashioned in their ways. I wasn't spoiled but I always knew that I was adored.'

How different their childhoods had been. 'You were lucky.'

'Why?'

'Not every child is wanted so much.'

She jerked back in her stool, her eyes wide in alarm. 'You mean our child?'

Was she serious? He dropped his water bottle down on the concrete counter with a thud. 'No. Of course not. I want this child—didn't today prove that to you? Why else would I have gone through with it?'

For the longest while she stared at him and then quietly answered, 'I appreciate the sacrifice you've made.'

He gritted his teeth, hating the hurt in her voice, and tried to steer their conversation back on track. They had to learn to work together, not constantly be tense and wary of one another. 'What excuse did you give to your parents for us not going on a honeymoon?'

'I said that we planned on going away later in the pregnancy, when I was feeling less poorly.'

He placed both hands on the breakfast counter and scanned her face for any signs of illness. 'Are you unwell? I thought your nausea had gone.'

'It comes and goes but it's nothing serious. I had to find an excuse for us not having a honeymoon.'

'You must tell me if you're feeling ill.'

Her expression tightened. 'Out of concern for the baby?'

He reined in his disquiet at the angry hurt in

her voice that he was guilty of causing by recklessly sleeping with her and said, 'For you too.' He moved towards her. 'You're my wife, Charlotte.' It was his first time saying that. My wife.

A blush formed on her cheeks and a knot formed in his heart.

She smiled nervously. 'I have something I want to give to you.' She paused and worried her lip. 'It's a wedding present of sorts.'

She got up and walked back out into the hallway where her suitcase lay. His driver had collected it from her apartment earlier that morning prior to the wedding ceremony. All of her other items were to be delivered by a removal company tomorrow.

When she came back she stood by the breakfast bar and stared down at the small piece of paper in her hands.

Slowly, almost reluctantly, she passed it to him along the surface of the counter separating them.

The photograph-sized light piece of paper held a black and white image. He stared at it not understanding.

His heart began to thud.

He picked it up and swallowed hard.

He could just make out the image of a head, a long body, curled up legs.

In the distance, he heard Charlotte say, 'It's a sonogram of our baby.'

Confused, he looked up sharply, 'When did you get this?'

She gave him a pensive smile. 'Wednesday, when I went for my twelve-week scan and obstetrician appointment at the Claremont.'

He stared at her in disbelief. They had had a heated discussion a few weeks back as to where her maternity care should take place. Charlotte had intended attending a hospital close to her old apartment but he wanted her care to be closer by. The Claremont, located only a five-minute drive away from here, was world-renowned for its consultant-led maternity care. Charlotte had eventually given into his arguments why she should attend the Claremont, but was this exclusion of him her way of getting him back for his insistence that he have an equal say in her maternity care? 'Why didn't you tell me? Shouldn't the father go too?'

'You weren't around.'

Angry that she had excluded him, angry at no longer feeling in control of his life, he waved the piece of paper at her. 'You should have told me. I should have been there with you.'

She reached up and pulled the white silk flower from her hair. 'You spend most of your time trying to avoid me.'

'What do you mean? I called you every day while I was away.'

Patting her hair, she gave a resigned shrug. 'Since our engagement you've been away constantly. If you're as absent as this when the baby is born our marriage won't survive.'

Thrown, he fought back. 'I've given you my word that I won't be absent. I *will* be there for my child.'

'We'll see.'

Her unconvinced, resigned tone dissolved his righteous anger.

Which was replaced with a heavy dose of guilt.

She was right.

He had been avoiding her.

Unconsciously needing time away, the distraction of work to bury the dread of messing up with his child...with his wife.

Not trusting himself around her.

Not trusting himself not to kiss her and a whole lot more.

He had to change. She and the baby deserved better.

He went and fetched his phone from the kitchen table where he had dropped it earlier. 'When's your next appointment?'

'I have my twenty-week scan on July fourteenth.'

He angled away from her and inhaled deeply. Old memories of his parent's broken promises to celebrate the French National holiday of Independence together as a family tugged hard in his chest. Instead he would join his best friend Yann's family to celebrate, their warm welcome only emphasising the coldness of his own home. Without turning he mindlessly scrolled through his phone calendar and said, 'Bastille Day.'

'Do you go back to France to celebrate it?' Without waiting for his answer, she said in a rush, 'I can go to the scan by myself. It won't be a problem.'

She didn't want him at the scan.

When was she going to understand that he wanted to be a full participant in this pregnancy? He *was* the father. With rights and responsibilities.

He turned back to her and through gritted teeth asked her for the time of the scan appointment and entered it into his phone.

He had fifty-seven unread emails. He should look at them. He normally would still be working at this time on a Friday night.

His new wife looked at him, perplexed.

Freezing her out, going to his home office to work, would clearly be counterproductive. They needed to work on their relationship—his last marriage failed because they never spoke properly, never were clear in what they could give to the other person, or what they expected of one another.

He was not making that mistake with this marriage.

Reluctantly he dropped his phone back onto the counter. 'I left France when I was twenty. I was offered an apprenticeship with a German construction company. I've only returned to France since for business reasons.'

'Do you miss it?'

'I guess.'

'Do you ever think of returning, living there?'

'I haven't thought about it. I grew up in the Charente region amongst the vineyards. I guess I miss the open spaces there, the slower pace of life. When I was growing up I used to dream of owning my own vineyard.'

Yann's family had owned a vineyard; their fifteenth-century chateau set in the centre of the property had been filled with endless love, laughter and acceptance.

Back then, he had thought that one day he too might be able to create his own world of family and love and belonging when he was older.

But the bitterness of his first marriage had shown him just how ridiculous those dreams had been.

He was just as incapable as his parents of selflessly loving a partner, of not sabotaging it all.

Charlotte gave a light laugh. 'I used to dream of being a tortoise. I thought it would be so cool to be able to carry my house around on my back!' Shaking her head in playful mockery of her childhood dream, she added, 'At least your dream is still feasible.'

No, it wasn't feasible.

He wasn't capable of the selfless love that a marriage demanded.

And now he was married to a woman who didn't trust him, who didn't want to marry him in the first place.

And she was right not to trust him.

Look at how he destroyed his first marriage.

Shame pulled like a tight fist in his chest; he took a slug of his water, the bubbles popping harshly at the back of his throat.

'Maybe one day you'll take our baby to France. Show her where you grew up.'

Taken aback by her suggestion, he stared at her.

And despite the painful memories of his childhood with his parents, there was so much he loved and still missed about his childhood home place, the endless fields of vineyards and sunflowers, swimming in the meadow-lined Charente River with his school friends, the trips to La Rochelle, climbing Dune du Pilat in Arcachon.

But would going back just be a painful reminder of all the hurt and the constant, twisting, painful knowledge that he wasn't wanted? That he wasn't loved.

He shook off those thoughts and narrowed his eyes, challenging her insistence that the baby was a girl. 'I'm sure *he'd* love it.' His throat tightened and he asked, 'Did you find out the sex of the baby at the scan?'

She lifted a hand to rest on her stomach. 'No. I want to keep it a surprise until the birth.' She gave him a cautious look. 'Is that okay with you?'

He nodded in agreement, his heart hammering at how tantalising his new bride looked in her white gown, perched on the breakfast stool, her hand cradling his unborn son.

He had been avoiding her.

The least he could do was apologise. 'My first marriage ended over fifteen years ago. I haven't been in a serious relationship since. Our relationship…our marriage, it's all so new. Give me some time to get things right.'

Charlotte nodded but she was clearly still unconvinced. And looked rather sad at that fact.

He shifted on his feet. 'I want this to work out.'

Her sombre eyes held his. 'I guess you need to prove it now.'

Hating her wariness, her doubt, even if they were justified, he lifted up the sonogram picture and studied it deliberately. 'It takes two to make a marriage work. We clearly need to establish how we communicate. How we work together. But most important of all is that we start as we mean to go along, in every aspect of our relationship.'

'Meaning?'

'Meaning no more surprises like today. We take decisions together as a couple, and that includes the pregnancy. I want to be present at all appointments. Plus we need to meet at least once a day to talk.'

'That won't be a problem for me.' Her tight tone implied that it would prove to be a problem for him.

They regarded each other cagily.

The distance between them once again thrown into sharp relief.

He planted his hands on his hips. 'Nor me.'

Her head dropped to the side, a sceptical eyebrow raised. 'Fine, let's have breakfast every morning.'

He dropped his hands from his hips. 'I go to the gym at six.'

'At seven so.'

He met with his PA every morning at seven. His day would be a nightmare if he started any later. 'I go straight to work.'

She let out a disbelieving breath.

Raising his hands in surrender, he said, 'Okay, we'll have breakfast at seven.'

She gave a satisfied nod. 'When the baby is born I expect you to be home by seven at the latest. For now I'll accept you being home by eight.'

He loosened his tie and opened his top shirt button. How was he going to manage the demands of work with this new domestic regime? For now he countered her proposition with a more feasible figure. 'Nine.'

She pursed her lips, a combative spirit emboldening the brightness in her eyes. 'I thought we were going to set a routine.'

'Eight-thirty.'

She shook her head and sighed dramatically as though terribly disappointed.

Dieu! She was enjoying this.

She gave him a tight smile. 'Until September, after that we'll pull it back each week by half an hour until it's seven. And with regards to travel, you'll have to cut that back too. The baby will need her father here. I'm happy to accept you travelling for two weeks a month until September and after that a week per month.'

She was testing his resolve to put the baby first.

Well, two could play at that game. 'Fine. If we're going to be so prescriptive in setting our daily routine then we should do the same with our sleeping arrangements. We'll sleep in the same bedroom.'

He moved away, ignoring her aghast expression, and added, 'Starting tonight. You look tired. I'll take your suitcase up to our bedroom.'

Charlotte chased after Lucien up the three flights of stairs that led to his top-floor bedroom suite, abandoning her shoes on the first floor.

Averting her eyes from his super-king-size bed, she followed him into his adjoining dressing room and watched him deposit her luggage onto a suitcase rack. She gave a disbelieving laugh. 'You're actually serious, aren't you?'

'*Absolument*. Absolutely. Our baby will not grow up in a house with parents who sleep in separate bedrooms.'

'Why not?'

'What type of message would it give if we sleep in separate rooms? I'm assuming you want our child to believe we're in love too?'

He had a point. But still, this was crazy. They couldn't sleep in the same bed. 'Yes, but—'

'And what about my housekeeper—what is she to think? And your parents when they visit and see that we're sleeping apart?'

'I'll say that I'm not sleeping well at the moment, which is the truth.'

'*Pour l'amour du ciel!* For heaven's sake, Charlotte, as if they are going to believe that a young and healthy couple who are supposedly in love would want to sleep apart.'

She stared at him aghast and then blankly down at her suitcase.

He was right…to a point.

But she also knew he was testing her.

Testing her continual assertions that she was committed to raising their baby in a happy, loving environment, while at the same time being sceptical of his pledges to do likewise.

It would be excruciating to have to share his bed.

To have to lie there and try not to remember their night together and how she had responded to him. How she had cried out in pleasure. Time and time again.

But there was no way she was going to admit any of that to him and she certainly wasn't going to give him the satisfaction of calling her bluff.

She bent down and twisted the suitcase to face her and opened it, the lid flying backwards. 'You want us to sleep in the same bed. Fine. Just stay to your side of the bed.'

He stepped towards her and she forced herself not to move.

He brought with him his scent, the pull of his large body, the memories of her nipping at the tender skin at the base of his throat the last time she had been in this bedroom suite.

His head dropped until only inches separated them. 'I promise to be a gentleman at all times.'

A deep shiver ran through her at his softly spoken words.

She fisted her hands and dared to look up and into his eyes. Eyes that held a hint of mischief but also shared intimate memories.

Her heart came to a standstill.

Crushed by how much she still wanted him,

crushed by knowing it could never happen again, crushed by her deep craving to have him stare with the same want and tenderness as he had that cold March night, she lashed out, 'I'm already paying the consequences of our poor judgement. I don't think it's something we should repeat.'

He jerked back.

His mouth hardened.

Intense impersonal icy green eyes held hers. 'You're right. It was ill-judged. And I'm sorry that you're having to pay the cost of my lack of judgement.' He moved beyond her and added, 'I'm going for a shower. I'll leave you to unpack.'

Once inside the bathroom he shut the door with a heavy thud.

Charlotte dropped her head and ran her hands tiredly over her face, drawing in a deep breath.

Sleeping in the same bed was his idea—surely he didn't expect her to embrace it without argument?

She hesitated for a moment at the suitcase but then began to unpack, her thoughts alternating from agreeing with his reasoning to wondering if she was losing her mind. A constant thought worming its way through her mind—was getting her to sleep in his bed some scheme to manipulate her?

Had he another agenda other than keeping up the pretence of their marriage.

Was she being manoeuvred and controlled by a master tactician…for purposes that she couldn't even start to understand?

Was she way out of her depth without realising it?

It was another ten minutes before he emerged from the bathroom.

She jumped up guiltily from where she had been waiting on the side of the bed.

One glance in his direction and her throat went drier than the ginger biscuits she was still having to eat to keep her now early morning nausea at bay.

She clutched her bundle of nightclothes and toiletries closer to her. 'I'll…ahem… I'll…' Heat bunched in her cheeks.

He did not say a word but walked towards the dressing room, wearing nothing but a white towel slung low on his hips.

She swallowed at the sight of a large drop of water that was slowly travelling down the length of his tanned muscular back, the outline of his bottom beneath the towel, the shape of his calves.

His wet hair was slicked back, the colour now a much darker shade, just like his mood.

She placed her bundle onto a bathroom stool and reluctantly went back outside and stood close to the dressing-room door. 'I need help with my dress.'

His large frame, now dressed in only wine-coloured cotton pyjama bottoms, soon filled the doorway.

She twisted away from the menace in his expression. Her back to him, she explained, 'I can't undo the buttons.'

She waited for him to respond. The silent chasm between them laying bare the reality of their marriage on what *should be* a unique, intimate and special night between a husband and wife.

A groom should happily undress his bride.

She shivered when he walked behind her, his height and size dwarfing hers.

She crossed her arms and closed her eyes.

One by one his fingers released the buttons.

She squeezed her eyes more firmly shut. Pushing away the desire to turn to him. Pushing down on the giddy butterflies in her tummy thanks to the skim of his slightly calloused fingers on her skin. Pushing away the memories of that night they were together and how he had fervently undressed her, and how cruelly it compared to his detached, controlled unbuttoning now.

Would she ever get used to not being truly wanted, to not being desired?

To being in a marriage that only existed because they had conceived a child together.

When he had reached as far as her waist, she stepped away and muttered with her back still to him, 'I can manage the rest,' and scuttled into the bathroom.

Inside she locked the door and undressed, her whole body trembling.

After a quick shower, she brushed her teeth, rehearsing in her mind the plan for when she got into bed with him. She would be polite. Say goodnight. Turn on her side. And fall asleep.

It didn't need to be anything more complicated or dramatic than that. They were both grown adults with a child to raise.

But having finished brushing her teeth, she stupidly became undone again.

Where should her toothbrush live?

In the holder next to Lucien's?

It seemed too intimate. Too permanent.

Tears blinded her for a moment.

And just how lonely she was going to be in this marriage hit her hard.

She was about to make a life with a man who only married her because she was carrying his baby.

She would never have the bond, intimacy, attachment or trust her parents shared.

But your baby will have a father. Isn't that enough for you?

She plonked her toothbrush into the holder and twisted away.

And twisted back, shoving it as far away from Lucien's as possible.

Outside in the bedroom he was sitting up in bed, reading a book, unfairly displaying his naked and formidable tanned chest, taut with powerfully defined pecs and a mind-blowing six-pack. She had kissed each of those muscles on that night, her lips slowly moving over the beautifully juxtaposed smooth skin and hard muscle beneath.

She skirted to the other side of the bed.

He lowered the hardback tome he was reading, his gaze wandering over her dark leggings and baggy yoga sweater. 'Going to the gym?'

'I get cold during the night.' She lay down in the bed, switched off her light and, clinging to the edge of her side of the bed, said, 'Goodnight.'

Long slow minutes ticked by.

Behind her she heard no movement.

'I meant it earlier when I said I won't touch you.'

Her heart was pumping faster than it ever did in her weekly spinning classes. Her throat was stupidly dry once again. She eventually managed to say, 'I know.'

Lucien plunged the room into darkness by switching off his bedside lamp. 'Goodnight, Charlotte.'

She bit her lip.

It would be okay.

She would fall asleep soon.

And she had Lucien here to protect her.

Or was he scarier than the dark?

'Lucien?'

'Yes?'

'Would you mind if I put on the bathroom light? I don't like sleeping in the dark.'

He didn't say anything for a few minutes. He was probably too busy asking himself why he had ever thought that marriage was a good idea.

On a loud exhale he got out of the bed.

She twisted onto her back.

His footsteps were barely audible on the carpeted floor.

Instead of the main light he switched on the shaving light over the sink mirror.

When he rejoined her in the bed she whispered, 'Thank you.'

He didn't say anything in response.

She cringed, certain now that he was majorly hacked off.

She thought he had fallen asleep when he suddenly said, 'How come the dark wasn't an issue the last time you slept here?'

Without thinking she admitted, 'I was too exhausted to notice.'

There was a moment of silence and she died inside.

But then he chuckled.

And she giggled in relief and mortification.

But their light laughter quickly died.

To be replaced by tight tension that filled the room.

Was he remembering their endless lovemaking as she was?

Even now, leaving her pregnancy aside, which she would never ever regret, she would never be sorry that she had slept with Lucien. It had been too special. It had held an almost dreamlike quality. It was as if they had been two different people, happy to find each other for a few incredible hours where only they existed. It had been intense, beautiful, extraordinary.

He deserved to know the truth of how she felt about that night. What she had said earlier had sounded all wrong. 'You said earlier that you were sorry about our night together... I wanted that night to happen as much as you did. I knew what I was doing.'

The mattress sagged a little as he moved. She twisted her head to see him gazing in her direction.

'I'm your CEO. I should have known better.'

'But it just happened...it's just one of those things. Nobody's to blame.' That night, they hadn't had a hope of stopping such intense, insane chemistry and attraction.

'There was a point in the garden when you looked unsure. We should have stopped then.'

'I didn't want to.' She paused and knew he deserved a better explanation. 'I was hurt in the past, that's why I was unsure. It had nothing to do with you.'

'Who hurt you?'

She scrunched her eyes shut. This was something she didn't want to speak about.

Could their wedding night be more different from the norm? A gap you could drive a double-decker bus through between them in their bed. No shared history or reference points. She didn't even know what his favourite food was, the type of movies he liked to watch.

'When I was twenty-two my then boyfriend cheated on me with my best friend.'

'Ouch.'

'Exactly.'

Silence fell on the room again.

She twisted her head. Across the expanse of the bed, Lucien was watching her with a frown.

Her heart ricocheted around her chest.

It felt so right yet so wrong to be lying here with him.

'You loved him?'

She blinked hard at his question, the gentleness of his tone puncturing through all the defences she had spun around herself these past six years. For the first time she admitted to herself just what she had lost back then.

Through a knotted throat she confessed, 'With all of my heart.'

Lucien looked away, his focus now on the ceiling above him. 'Did you try getting back together?'

'There was no point. Even I could tell how deeply in love they were. They're now happily married with three children by all accounts.'

In the resumed silence of the room, she stared at the silhouette of the modern gold and crystal chandelier that hung at the centre of the ceiling, feeling totally exposed, wondering why she had told him all of this.

Did he pity her?

Did he understand what it was like to have a broken heart?

Would he think her weak?

Be more wary of her?

After all, he only knew her as a coolly detached, logical professional. He was probably recoiling at this much too personal and emotional conversation.

She should say something to end the silence, reassure him that she wasn't a complete emotional wreck. Erect the barriers around herself once again.

But before she could do so, he spoke. 'It still hurts?'

His question was asked without judgement. Was

there a hint of understanding? In a quiet voice she said, 'Yes.'

Oh, why was she talking to him like this?

She never spoke to anyone about what had happened between her and Dan. Preferring to consign it to a bitter lesson learned in life, not to be revisited.

'I'm sorry you had to go through that…what your ex did was unforgivable.' Why did he sound so angry, so vehement?

'I guess.'

'You sound like you forgive him.'

Did she? 'No… I don't know.'

He waited for her to speak but she didn't know what to say. How would she explain to her new husband that Dan, that entire year of being ill, had shaken her to the core? Had ripped away the happy person she once had been. And left her floundering as to who she could trust and annoyed at her own naivety in believing that love could conquer all. Annoyed for thinking you could rely on others for support and care when ultimately there was only one person you could count on: yourself.

A truth she had to remember in this marriage.

Lucien was her husband but in name only. All she could hope for was that he would be a good father to her child. 'I just wished I had known at the time that nothing stays the same in life… I thought I'd be in pain for ever.'

'How are you doing now?'

His quietly spoken question sounded so genuine, so caring that for a moment she actually
wanted to cry. But she pushed aside the heavy
weight of emotion jamming her throat to answer.
'I'm okay. How about you? Are you getting used
to the idea of being a father?'

A husband?

He shrugged one of those impossibly wide
shoulders. 'A little. How about you being a mum?'

'I'm daunted, to be honest. I'm trying not to
think about giving birth. And I'm even more worried about taking care of something so tiny after.
I've barely ever held a baby. I've never fed one, or
changed a nappy.'

'I'm the same. Maybe we should both do a parenting course. My trainer on the How to be a Good
Husband course highly recommended a holistic
retreat that encourages a birthing-in-the-woods-
while-chanting approach. We could give that a go.'

Despite herself, she giggled and the sudden bub-
ble of happiness that floated in her chest grew bigger when she saw the teasing mischief glinting in
his eyes. If only their relationship could always be
as relaxed as this. 'You know, hanging out with
you mightn't be so bad after all.'

The room grew still.

His gaze worked from her eyes down to her
mouth.

She couldn't read his blank expression.

A reckless urge to move towards him, to place her hand on his exposed chest, to feel his taut, warm skin, the tightness of the muscle beneath, to inhale him, to connect with him in the most potent and powerful way a man and woman could do so swept through her.

A dangerous charge whipped around the room.

It would be so easy to reach out. To touch her fingers to his arm. To invite him to move towards her.

Desire and need coiled tight inside her but she forced herself to say, 'I think we should go to sleep.'

His answer was a quick nod and he turned away from her.

And the loneliness of her new marriage hit her again. An empty, hollow sensation pumping through her heart.

Dieu! He was such a hypocrite.

Lucien stared at his bedside clock and gritted his teeth.

Two hours after they had said goodnight to one another and sleep still eluded him thanks to the desire, anger, irritation swirling inside him.

He wanted to track down Charlotte's ex and make him pay for causing her such obvious pain.

But at the same time he wanted to move across the bed and make love to her, to drive away all those memories of her ex. To recreate the passion of their one night together. To hear her hold her breath time and time again and the explosion of sound as she responded to him.

What a hypocrite.

He wanted to punish her ex while at the same time thinking and wanting to act in a way that would cause her even greater hurt in the long-term by complicating the delicate truce they had set in place to raise their child together.

A bigger hypocrite because he had behaved much more despicably than her ex in the past. In an act that had confirmed that he was as weak willed and lacking in honour as his father.

He needed to be careful. Already he was feeling a closeness to Charlotte. Her stubborn, sharp-witted, vibrant personality beneath that detached image was getting to him. Weakening his resolve that he would keep his distance from her. And now that he knew of her past, he had an even greater urge to protect her from any other hurt. The irony being, of course, that he would have to protect her from himself.

His first marriage had quickly descended into endless rows and frustration as they had realised that passion and a shared love for partying could not sustain their relationship and the responsibilities they had needed to face in life. But they had been so entwined emotionally, so believing that the other person would save them from a life of loneliness, so invested in each other, that their break-up had been both brutal and cruel as they had tried to extract themselves from their passionate and all-consuming marriage.

This marriage could not be like that. He had to keep his distance from Charlotte. For her sake. For the baby's sake. For his own sake.

He turned in the bed.

His heart karate-chopped against his chest.

Charlotte was awake and staring in his direction.

He wanted to move towards her. To touch the long length of her hair that looked like silver threads in the dark shadows of the room. To kiss that soft, beautiful mouth. To make her his.

Wasn't that what was supposed to happen on your wedding night? Long glorious hours of lovemaking.

Instead he forced himself to ask, like any dutiful father-to-be, 'Is everything okay? Can I get you something? A glass of water?'

She shook her head and turned away.

He flipped onto his back.

Feeling more alone than ever.

CHAPTER SIX

TWO WEEKS LATER Charlotte roamed a Mayfair art gallery on Cork Street, trying to avoid actually looking at the exhibition of modernist paintings that were threatening to turn her hovering headache into a full-blown migraine.

At the rear of the room, standing next to a particularly lurid painting full of lime green and yellow splatters and daubs, Lucien was deep in conversation with Selina Hutton, the only current female chairperson of a UK investment bank.

Earlier when Charlotte had spoken to Selina as they had both puzzled over the meaning of a twisted steel sculpture, Selina had been charming and funny. And at forty, she was not only strikingly good-looking but carried the easy confidence of a woman perfectly content in her own skin. Her fitted ankle-length teal trousers and loose cream silk blouse hung perfectly on her trim body, her mane of chestnut hair holding just the right amount of bounce and glossiness.

Charlotte turned away from them. And pulled on her black shift dress. Suddenly feeling invisible.

She fanned herself with the exhibition price list. And sneaked a look back towards Lucien.

His slim-fitting white shirt over wheat-coloured

chinos unwittingly revealed her Achilles' heel: his sharp broad shoulders and ridiculously defined torso that were reducing her to feverish insomnia every night.

And she was completely hacked off about it.

Couldn't he at least once in a while go to bed before her? Spare her the sight of him emerging from the bathroom night after night, freshly showered and pyjama bottoms slung low on his hips.

While she pretended to be asleep.

Which was a joke. Because she lay awake each night reliving their night together.

The way her heart had spun in wonder.

Memories of how he had looked at her with such passionate amazement.

As though he would never tire of her.

As though it had all been special.

How foolish she had been.

For two weeks now they had been sleeping together. And keeping to his word, he had proved to be the perfect gentleman.

He had tired of her after one single night.

Okay, so maybe that was a little unfair.

If they hadn't been CEO and employee in the first instance, if she hadn't ended up pregnant, maybe the fire between them would have been able to burn a little longer. But it would have burned out eventually.

Lucien would have wanted to move on.

And so would she.

Wouldn't she?

Lucien turned in her direction. His gaze moved down over her.

The fire of want and embarrassment pulled hard inside her.

She ducked behind a pillar.

What did he think when he looked at her? Did he find her ever-growing belly, how her entire body seemed to be softening into lush curves, un-attractive? Did he wonder what on earth he had done in marrying her?

She tried to ignore a tearing sensation in her heart.

Why did she even care?

Her headache was worsening.

She needed air.

She needed to get away from the sight of Lucien and Selina flirting together.

An hour later, Charlotte meandered her way around the Mayfair square that led to her new home, still struggling to fathom how her life had changed direction so dramatically since she had rung in the New Year with her parents less than six months ago.

Back then, as they had watched the village fire-works together, her biggest worry had been how she was going to secure her next promotion.

Now she had childbirth, being a mother, and being a wife to the sexiest man she had ever met but who was blind to her to worry about.

The worst part was that instead of being attracted to Lucien she should be furious with him.

He wasn't meeting half of the promises he had agreed to.

Placing her key in the lock of the front door, she cursed the fact that she was allowing her attraction to him to get in the way of all her usual good sense and logic.

Lucien was a heartbreaker, a go-getter who liked novelty, who could make you feel as if you were the most special, most cherished woman in the world until the next woman came along.

She had known so many like him in university, dating them in her first few years there. She had allowed herself to be charmed by them, forgiven them when she should have booted them out of her life, and invariably ended up hurt and humiliated when they had dumped her for someone else.

That was why she'd fallen for Dan. He had seemed so different. So genuine.

And he had been kind and generous, until she had become ill.

And now she was foolishly falling for Lucien's charm and allowing herself to be blind to the fact that he was full of empty promises.

'Where were you?' Lucien stalked down that hallway towards her.

She gripped her milkshake carton tighter. 'I went for a walk.'

He gave her an infuriated stare. 'Why didn't you tell me that you were leaving the gallery?'

'You were busy chatting to Selina Hutton.'

'So? You could have interrupted us.' He lifted both hands in exasperation. 'You're my partner, my wife, you don't just walk out without telling me. I felt ridiculous having to ask others if they had seen you. And you didn't answer your phone when I called you.'

She opened her clutch bag and lifted her phone to see seven missed calls from him. 'My phone was on silent. There's some problems with the Estonia project I'm working on that I wanted to think through by going for a walk.'

He didn't respond but looked at her with a disbelieving frown. In the excruciating silence that followed, her skin heated uncomfortably as those green eyes studied her unflinchingly. Eventually, unable to handle his stare any longer, she mumbled, 'I was feeling ill. I needed some air.'

He shook his head and turned around while muttering, 'And a milkshake apparently.'

She followed him into the lounge that had a double-height bay window overlooking the residents-only park set at the centre of the square.

Lucien stood in front of the large marble fireplace, his stiff and menacing reflection showing in the gilt mirror hanging above it. 'Why didn't you tell me that you were feeling ill?'

'It didn't look as though you'd appreciate being disturbed in your conversation with Selina.'

His eyes narrowed and he drew his shoulders back. 'You don't trust me, do you?'

She swallowed hard.

This was the first time she'd ever seen him this angry, this cold and formidable.

Deep down she knew she should be reasonable, make allowances for the demands and pressure of his position at work, but the foolish pain within her that he didn't find her attractive, the loneliness of her marriage, her ongoing fears for what type of father and son-in-law he would be, the loss of her own independence had her say bitterly, 'Let's see. You agreed that we'd meet for breakfast every day. This week you made it twice. You were home when it was past ten o'clock, three nights. I barely see you. Everything seemed to be working so well our first week together but in the past week it's all falling apart. I'm honestly questioning your commitment to this marriage, to our baby.'

Lucien tried to breathe deeply into his lungs, fighting to steady his heart, to shake off the adrenaline still coursing through his veins.

He had been angry and humiliated when he'd realised she had left the gallery.

And guilty, because he had been avoiding her all evening, trying to keep a firm hold on how much he wanted to place his hand on her growing stomach, how sexy she looked this evening with her hair hanging loose, a bold *come and get me* slash of red lipstick on her mouth. How much he wanted to run his hands over her curves, the warmth of her naked beauty again.

With each passing day he was growing more and more attracted to her. In their first week together, when he'd got home from work in the evenings he had often found her on the living-room floor practising yoga or on the sofa, curled up reading a book. She shouldn't have looked sexy dressed in her yoga wear, her hair tied back into a messy ponytail. But she had. And when she'd smiled in his direction and asked if he wanted something to drink, to eat, in that first week he had said yes, please. Which had been a big mistake. Because in those few short days his attraction, need for her, had gone shooting off the Richter scale as they'd chatted over food, as they'd washed up over supper.

And then he would have to feign nonchalance when they went upstairs, pretend that he didn't see the shape and swell of her body beneath her light cotton pyjamas. Maybe it would have been better if she had stuck to wearing her gym clothes in bed.

And the following morning as she had yawned over breakfast, her make-up-free skin pink from sleep, he would have to leave for work tense with the desire to kiss her. And twice they had attended work meetings together and his concentration had been shot to pieces. In one meeting with his board, Charlotte had made a presentation on the funding due diligence for a port construction project in Estonia. He had watched his astute wife handle the assertive questioning of the board with pride, and with vastly inappropriate thoughts of how he would like to get her alone in the boardroom and strip her bare before making love to her.

Last week, knowing he had to create distance between them before he did something he'd regret, he had started coming home later, the ever looming demands of work giving him a legitimate justification.

The same justification he had used tonight when he had spoken to Selina Hutton about his plans for Huet when in truth all he had wanted to do was take Charlotte by the hand and walk through the summer streets of London with her. Perhaps walk to St James's Park, hire a deckchair, eat ice cream. Chat and argue with her. Laugh with her. Kiss her.

His anger that Charlotte had walked out on him

had flicked to panic when he had arrived home to find the house empty.

With each unanswered phone call that panic had intensified. Images of her falling in those sexy high-heeled red sandals she had insisted on wearing tonight persecuting him as he had waited and waited and waited for her to return.

He had feared for the baby. For her.

He knew he should walk away, get his emotions under control. But the rage, the panic still in him had him growl out, 'This is exactly why I never wanted to marry again. Stupidly arguing and pulling each other apart. Never being able to satisfy the other person.'

With her long blonde wavy hair hanging loose about her face she looked incredibly young and sweet…the exception being the sharp fury firing from her sea-green eyes. She folded her arms, her mouth twisting. 'I wouldn't be bringing any of this up if I thought you were even trying—for crying out loud, last weekend when my parents visited you were completely withdrawn and it was obvious that you resented them being here in your house. I spent the whole afternoon trying to pretend all was happiness and light between us. I was actually glad when you said that you had to go into the office.'

'It's your house too. And, no, I didn't resent them being here. That's just a ludicrous idea.' He paused and thought back to their visit, the laughter between them, the baskets of food her mum had arrived with, their fussing over Charlotte, their pride in her.

And he had felt like a fraud.

They thought he was in love with her.

They thought he would do everything in his power to protect her.

When in truth he wanted to wreck her heart, their baby's future, by sleeping with her again, by growing closer to her, getting to know her, which would confuse the basis of their relationship, cause misunderstandings, create emotional bonds he would eventually tear apart.

And if he managed to keep his distance emotionally and physically, if he protected her heart by keeping himself distant, there was still no guarantee that he would be a good father to their child.

Was Charlotte's lack of trust in him, the fact that she was constantly judging him, justified? Was he proving to be as irresponsible and self serving as his parents?

Because surely he should be man enough to be able to push his attraction to her aside, to fulfil his side of the bargain to be a responsible husband and father.

Now, the anger in her eyes was burning less brightly, and a hurt expression was rising up instead.

He hated to see her upset, a raw pain he didn't understand pierced his chest, and words exploded out of him. 'I don't know how to act when you're with your parents. I'm overwhelmed by the love between you.'

He backed away. Stunned at his own words.

Charlotte came towards him. 'I don't understand.'

He looked away. Fighting the temptation to walk out of the room.

The only other person he had ever described his past to was his first wife. And she had used it like a weapon when their marriage had ended, accusing him of being as weak willed as his own father, shouting that he was no different and would always be greedy and self-centred in any relationships.

Did he want to give Charlotte that power?

But maybe if she understood his past she'd know to stay away from him.

He went and stood at the bay window and stared out at the street and park beyond.

When he turned back, Charlotte was still! in the same spot, waiting for him to speak.

'My upbringing was the polar opposite of yours. You said yours was full of happiness and love—well, I spent my childhood trying to appease my parents, constantly trying to stop their arguments.'

Trying to make them love me.

His stomach rolled in distaste at what he was about to say but the earlier surge of adrenaline because of his panic over her disappearance from the gallery drove him on recklessly. 'When I was fifteen I arrived home early one day and found my father in bed with a work colleague. My father refused to admit it to my mum so I had to tell her. She didn't believe me, said that I was lying. Until she saw them together herself one day at a café. She threw him out and he moved to Spain with the other woman.'

He paused as Charlotte walked towards him.

He glanced out into the park beyond the iron railings on the opposite side of the road, to the ancient plane trees weighed down in their dark green summer foliage.

He had come so far from his childhood, but not in what was important.

His new wife should fully understand what type of person he was.

Then perhaps she would know not to have too many expectations of him, too many hopes. 'My mother couldn't cope with living on her own. I didn't help. I was angry all of the time and getting into trouble at school. She moved a boyfriend in with us. He threw a beer can at me one day for stealing his beer. It smashed into my head. We ended up fighting on the floor. Blood pumping from my head. My mother screamed at me for ruining her new shoes and threw me out. Probably deservedly so.'

When Charlotte didn't respond he looked towards her furiously.

But the angry words that were about to demand if she was disgusted to be married to a man with such an awful family history, when hers was so damn normal and lovely, died when he saw the sadness in her eyes.

A sadness that was matched by the gentle tone of her voice when she spoke. 'How old were you?'

'Seventeen.'

'You were still a child.'

He shook his head. He fully accepted his role in his estrangement from his mother. 'I was out of control.'

'Where did you go?'

'I moved to Bordeaux and quickly fell in with other troubled teenagers. We all lived in a derelict house. It's where I met my first wife, Gabrielle.'

Should he tell Charlotte about his ex…the relationship they'd had?

The need to share his past with her was burning inside him.

For the first time ever he wanted to speak out loud about that time, to try to make sense of his teenage past and how much he'd messed up.

'Gabrielle moved into the apartment a few months after I did. Her mum had just died, she never knew her dad. She had no one else to turn to. We thought we could fix each other's loneliness. But our initial love and hope turned to hurt when we realised we couldn't make life better for one another. We couldn't fix one another, repair the damage within us. We were both selfish, wrapped up in our own wants and needs, and blamed each other for our marriage crumbling. It lasted less than a year.'

There was more he should tell her—that last night when he had delivered the final fatal blow to their marriage.

But he couldn't bring himself to.

The shame and guilt of his actions were too overwhelming.

The shock, the agony, the torture, the anger of Gabrielle's betrayal with one of the other men who lived in the apartment. He had found them kissing, Gabrielle dressed in only her underwear, her dress strewn on the kitchen floor.

After he had confronted them and realised their affair had been going on for months he had gone out.

And got drunk.

And slept with Gabrielle's friend.

A pathetic, weak, contemptible act that showed he was as weak as his own father.

He had spent more than fifteen years trying

to distance himself from that selfish, egotistical person.

But he was still the same person at heart despite all of his achievements. 'I'm a selfish person, Charlotte. From a messed-up family.'

He fisted his hands in hopeful intention. 'But I will do my best to be a good father.'

His stomach churning, he added bitterly, 'I overheard my parents arguing one night and it was clear that they considered me a mistake. My mother was only twenty when she became pregnant with me. My parents resented me for tying them down, for burdening them.'

He drew in a breath, thrown by just how passionate he felt about what he was going to say, 'So help me God, my child will never feel like he's a mistake or a burden. I will try to be a good husband to you, but I will probably never be the husband you need.'

Outside the evening was disappearing into night, sucking all of the light out of the lounge. Before her, Lucien stood with a dark dignity.

How little she knew her husband.

She needed some time and space to think about what he'd said.

But most of all she wanted to comfort him, give him the care and respect that had been missing from his childhood. 'Would you like a cup of tea?'

He gave her a quizzical look and shrugged.

She led the way into the kitchen and made their tea in silence. She placed their cups and the teapot on the old oak farm kitchen table. Lucien's interior designer had chosen well in selecting the table; it lent a much-needed homely feel to the hard lines of the concrete and minimalist white kitchen.

Lucien sat at the head of the table, facing out into the garden, she to his side. The same places they sat at, each time they shared a meal. An arrangement that had happened naturally, evolved without discussion, just one of many small, outwardly couple-like behaviours so at odds with the frustrations and distance of their relationship.

She poured their tea and sipped hers before she spoke. 'I don't think you're selfish. You married me for your child. To give her security. A family. That's the most selfless, loving act possible.'

He shook his head, not buying her words. 'Is it, though? Or is this all about my ego? Is it a crazy macho need to protect my own that belongs to caveman times rather than the modern day? You're perfectly capable of raising a child. Maybe I should have left you to it.'

'I want my child to have her father in her life. Hearing you describe your past, I now understand just how difficult it must have been for you to marry me.' She paused, struggling to talk against the rock of emotion wedged in her throat. 'I'm really moved that you would do that for our child. You'll be a great dad.'

He sat back in his chair and inhaled deeply.

Rubbed his hand along the back of his neck. Looking as though he was trying to fight her words. Find a reason not to believe her. Eventually he said with a bitter twist to his voice, 'I'm making for a lousy husband, though.'

She shrugged. 'I'm not exactly making for a great wife either. Let's face it, you'd have been better off married to someone like Selina Hutton.'

'Why on earth would you say that?'

Wasn't that obvious to him? Selina Hutton, sensible and pragmatic, would be able to keep her emotions at bay for the greater good of the family unit. 'You'd have been the ultimate power couple.'

He drew back in his chair. 'Selina and I were talking business, that's all.' He arched his neck, loosening out some kink. 'I don't want to hurt you, Charlotte. I like you…but my past history shows that I mess up relationships. This is one relationship I can't afford to wreck.'

Charlotte nodded as he held her gaze.

It *was* pointless falling for this man.

She would only end up hurt and destroying any hope of them raising their child together in harmony.

Yet a burning need rebelled inside her; she wanted to throw caution to the wind and to lean

across the table and touch her fingers to the str
column of his neck, run her hand along the ha.
lines of his collarbone, touch her lips to the eve
ning shadow on his jawline, inhale his brain-
stupefying scent.

With a sage wisdom that was totally at odds
with her attraction to him, her need for him, she
said, 'Maybe we should try harder at being friends,
be more supportive of one another.'

He gazed at her for long scorching seconds.

Oh, to be held in his arms again if only for a
few minutes.

To feel his mouth on hers.

To lose herself to him. To his warmth and
strength. To have his eyes hold her heart in the
suspended time of care and comfort and promise.

Lucien cleared his throat. 'We can try.'

She pulled her mouth into the semblance of a
smile. 'They say the best relationships are those
founded on friendship.'

They smiled at each other.

Pained smiles that didn't reach their eyes.

Both knowing that there was so much more that
they wanted from each other.

CHAPTER SEVEN

CHARLOTTE TRIED TO open her eyes but the pain was too intense. It felt as if someone had poured acid onto her brain. The epicentre just beneath her right temple.

Lying on one of the living-room sofas, she wanted to cry.

But it would hurt too much.

She couldn't move.

She heard the front door open.

It was Lucien's housekeeper's day off. She knew she should be worried but in truth she didn't care if they were about to be burgled. As long as the burglars got her a cold press while rifling through the kitchen cupboards they were welcome to whatever they wanted.

Familiar-sounding footsteps bounded up the stairs.

She tried to call out but when she lifted her head the acid burrowed even deeper into her brain.

She pushed the heel of her hand against her right eye, trying to ease the pressure there.

Within minutes he was rushing back down the stairs, calling her name.

In a croaky voice, pain slaying every facial muscle, she called, 'I'm in here.'

His footsteps tapped, tapped, tapped furiously on the wooden floor. 'Simon told me that you had gone home ill. Why didn't you tell me?'

This time she whispered, hoping not to stir the beast of pain currently living in her brain. 'You were busy...you had your meeting with the government guys from Denmark.'

'Why are you lying here? Why not upstairs in bed?' His voice was now anxious, the anger gone.

'I couldn't make it...pain too bad.'

She heard him come closer, his hand rested on her arm. Soothing. 'Another migraine?'

'The worst yet.'

'I'll call my doctor.'

'No point, I can't take anything. I just need to sleep for a while. Later I need to go back into the office to work on a sub-contractor adjudication.'

'You're not going anywhere but your bed today. I'll carry you upstairs—you'll sleep better there.'

She should object. She knew she should. But the pain outweighed the guilt of being out of work sick and the thought of the warmth and comfort of her bed was too great to resist. And even more, she wanted to be held by him if only for a few minutes. 'Please...and sorry, I can't open my eyes. It hurts too much.'

With surprising ease he gently lifted her up.

Just minutes ago she had felt alone and vulnerable.

Now she wanted to weep in relief to have him here, to be minded, to be cared for.

Upstairs, he lowered her onto the cool cotton of their bed quilt and, before she had the chance to do so, pulled off her high-heeled work shoes.

Still unable to open her eyes, she waited for him to speak.

He cleared his throat. 'Do you want me to undress you?'

So many women would give their eye teeth to hear Lucien Duval ask that question of them. And here she was preferring if he would just lie down beside her and hold her. 'No, it's fine. I'd like a blanket, though.'

After he had placed a blanket over her, his hands tucking the sides against her body, she heard him close the shutters and the swoosh when he drew the heavy silk curtains together on all three Georgian sash windows.

She curled up onto her side, wincing as the acid tunnelled into her brain once again.

'I've dampened a face cloth. Would you like to use it?'

She made the tiniest movement with her head to indicate yes and croaked out, 'Lay it on my temple.'

He laid the cool cloth down against her skin and she gave an involuntary groan. 'That's so nice, thank you.'

'*Dieu!* I feel so responsible. It's awful to see you in such pain.'

His voice, which came from very close by, as though he was crouched down before her, sounded tortured. She wished she could open her eyes to see him, to reassure him. 'It's okay…it's nice to have you here.'

He repositioned the cloth on her temple and when he'd finished his hand slowly moved down, gently, soothingly, over her hair. 'I'm glad I'm here. What can I do?'

Lie down beside me, hold me. Tell me that all this will go away.

'I just need to sleep. I'll be fine. You go back to work.'

He didn't say anything for the longest while but eventually, repositioning the cloth against her skin, whispered, 'I'll be downstairs, but I'll check on you throughout the afternoon.'

'Go back to work. I know how important your meeting is.'

He lifted up the blanket to cover her shoulders. 'It's more important that I stay with you. Try to sleep. I'll be here if you need me.'

At the backs of her eyes she felt tears form. She nodded and hoped he would leave before they fell onto her cheeks. Lucien had said the words she had willed Dan to say all those years ago but never did.

'I'll be here if you need me.'

She curled up on her side even more, hugging her knees into her chest, allowing his low whisper, the comfort, the reassurance, the care it brought to lull her to sleep.

Later that evening, Charlotte sat on the side of their bed and blinked hard, trying to focus on the time showing on Lucien's bedside clock. She had been asleep for more than three hours.

Though groggy and light-headed, she made her way into the bathroom, sending up silent thanks that sleep had washed away the burning acid from her brain.

For a moment she considered locking the bathroom door, but to do so now seemed petty.

When she had moved in with Lucien she had locked the bathroom door behind her as an act of defiance. An act to exclude him, push him away from her.

A silent way of communicating that she didn't trust him.

But they had to trust one another. It was the only way this marriage was going to survive.

She couldn't spend the next couple of decades locking the bathroom door on him. No married couple did that, did they?

Her parents certainly didn't.

Was she being foolhardy though?

Was she lowering her defences around him too much?

Was she confusing his care and kindness and attention towards her as being about her, when in truth it was all about protecting his child?

She turned on the shower, undressed and stepped under the warmth of the water. She turned the temperature up high, needing to feel the heat on her tense shoulders.

Since the night in the gallery when she had left early, they had been working on 'being friends'. But the downside of opening up to one another and spending time together was that she was growing even more attracted to him.

Last night she had persuaded him to go to the cinema at the British Film Institute on Southbank to watch a Norwegian crime thriller. He had been reluctant at first, pointing out that they had a home cinema in the basement. But though his basement cinema was more luxurious than any commercial cinema, the idea of watching a film in the darkness all alone with him had been too much for her. And anyway, she liked being out with him, walking the life-affirming streets of London together. Window-shopping along Piccadilly. The vibrancy and chaos of Piccadilly Circus. It was easier to talk to him when they were walking side by side rather than facing each other. It was less

...ersonal, less distracting when his piercing gaze wasn't focused on her.

They had arrived early to the cinema.

As had a couple who had sat in front of them.

Of similar age to them, the couple had flirted and teased, completely at ease with one other. They had continually touched one another affectionately, whispered to one another, shared brief kisses.

Their intimacy had laughed at the awkwardness that still existed between her and Lucien. An awkwardness, a lack of connection that would be the hallmark of their marriage for ever.

And to see up close just how it really should be between a couple had left a hollowness deep inside her for the rest of the evening.

When she was with Lucien she always got a temporary high from laughing, arguing, getting to know him. But then, as she had last night, she would be pulled up with a reminder that their relationship was only one of co-parenting their child.

The same reminder that mocked her every night when they lay in bed together and her body hummed with the need for him to roll over and touch her. The need to move across the wide expanse of their bed. Touch her mouth to his. Feel his hands on her body. As her stomach grew larger, her breasts more tender, an acute need to be intimate with the father of her baby was destroying her. But she forced herself to hold back. To stay away from him. For their baby's sake. And because she knew the pain of a broken heart and dreams.

Knew just how much you could damage a relationship when you grew too close.

When you depended on the other person for strength.

She switched off the shower and quickly dried. In their dressing room, she pulled on a short-sleeved navy jersey dress. It clung a little too tightly, but this evening she needed comfort above all. She would need to go maternity-clothes shopping soon as her jeans and work clothes no longer fitted. She loved how her body was changing as her pregnancy progressed. She felt more sensual, more womanly...and occasionally she caught Lucien staring at her stomach, at her heavier breasts, with intimate heat in his eyes. But then he would look away and her heart would slam to a stop, bereft at his silence.

Back out in the bedroom she opened the curtains and shutters, and lifted up the bottom of one of the sash windows. Birdsong and the distant, constant hum of traffic greeted her. For a moment she paused and looked out at the church spires in the distance, the tall building cranes that brought constant renewal to this ever-changing city.

Sitting at her new dressing table, she began to

dry her hair. Lucien had surprised her with the dressing table earlier in the week. The Art Deco table had a delicate round mirror and a bronze-plated drawer at the front where she stored her lipsticks and eyeshadows. Two further drawers sat at either side of the table, before tapering down to colt-like legs tipped with silvered bronze on the feet.

A matching stool with similarly tapered legs and upholstered in a heavy cream wool fabric had arrived with the table when it was delivered by one of London's leading auction houses.

Even with her limited knowledge of the antique market she had realised that the table must have cost a great deal. Lucien had refused to allow her to return it, saying that she deserved to sit at something so pretty every day.

His words and indulgent smile had stupidly thrilled her and she had stopped arguing and accepted the gift with the grace it deserved.

She was slowly learning to pick her battles with her new husband.

Halfway through drying her hair, she switched off the drier with a smile when Lucien entered the room. He dropped a number of bright yellow department-store bags onto the bed.

She gave him a teasing smile. 'Been out shopping?'

He threw her a *What do you think*? look and

said, 'Whoever invented online shopping was a genius.'

He came closer and his eyes slowly trailed over her face, and for a brief second his hand touched against her shoulder. 'How are you feeling?'

She swallowed and tried to ignore how her heart was melting. 'Much better than your poor back, I bet.'

He gave her an indignant frown. 'I squat press the equivalent of two of you every morning.' His expression sobering, he considered her for a while, as though wanting to make certain she was better. 'I ordered in dinner—are you up to eating?'

'I'd kill for a milkshake right now.'

'*Dieu!* How can you say that to me...a Frenchman who loves good food? I've ordered in light food from Gallery—a beef consommé and steamed hake to follow.'

Gallery, one of London's top restaurants, was located only a five-minute walk away from Lucien's house. From what she could gather, until she had moved in and started cooking meals, he had ordered from them most nights when he was alone in London and not out entertaining.

She turned in her chair and folded her arms. 'Are you trying to avoid my cooking?'

'Now what gave you that idea? Those chickpea burgers last night were...interesting.'

Okay, so they had been on the dry side, but they were healthy…apparently.

'I'll leave you to finish.' He paused and gestured to the parcels. 'They are for you.'

Intrigued, she got up and opened the first bag.

Inside she found a cashmere-blend pale blue throw. She unfurled it on the bed, running her hands over the soft material. In the second bag she found a similar-coloured lounge top and bottoms. She shook her head, laughing. 'I keep telling you, it's a girl, not a boy.'

'If it's a girl I'll do every night feed for the first month.'

Her husband the risk-taker. 'Now that's fighting talk.' She folded up the blanket and opened the smaller third bag. Inside she found a month's supply of her favourite brand of vanilla caramel fudge. She lifted it up accusingly. 'I've noticed that my fudge has been disappearing from the pantry cupboard. Hands off these ones. They're all mine.'

Standing at the bedroom door, he propped his hand on the doorframe. 'I thought marriage is all about sharing.' A cheeky smile broke on his mouth.

And her legs almost gave way.

She playfully conceded, 'I'll allow you to have the occasional one.'

They stood there smiling for much too long.

Until it began to get awkward.

Until it felt as if this was how married couples should be together.

She gestured back to his gifts, needing to break the tension. 'The presents are great, thank you, but there really was no need.'

Lucien approached the bed again and lifted up the throw.

He shuffled it from hand to hand.

His eyes met hers.

'I hate to see you in pain.'

When he was like this it was impossible to resist him. It would be so easy to forget why they could never be a true couple.

She forced herself to look away and said with a laugh, 'You'd better not come to the birth so.'

A hint of something, worry or perhaps guilt, flickered in his eyes. 'I wouldn't miss it for the world. I've cleared my diary for that week.'

'I could go early or late.'

He shrugged and walked back towards the door. 'I'll have my plane on standby at all times. Come downstairs when you are ready. Dinner will be delivered in twenty minutes.'

Switching the hairdryer back on, she gazed at his gifts lying on the bed and then stared at her reflection.

Seeing for herself the heat of pleasure in her cheeks at his thoughtfulness.

He was a master at worming his way into her heart.

And at times, like now, she just wanted to give into it all, to allow herself to fall for him totally, to enjoy his company without constantly second-guessing him, second-guessing her own ability to cope with another love affair gone bad.

Later that night, Lucien rolled up the set of architectural drawings he'd had his chief architect work on for the past week. Each day the two men had met to revise the plans until Lucien was satisfied that they were perfect.

He had intended giving them to Charlotte last night but had pulled back after their trip to the cinema. Seeing the ease and intimacy of the couple in front of them, and Charlotte's quietness beside him as she had watched them, had brought home what he was denying her by their marriage.

She had claimed that she had never wanted to marry, wanting to focus on her career instead. But it was obvious that her break-up with her ex was the true reason why she shied away from relationships.

With time she would probably have met a man capable of breaking down her defences and teaching her how to love again. But he had denied her that opportunity by marrying her.

Now she would never have the intimacy, the true closeness of a love marriage.

Guilt at that realisation and at how his attraction to her was getting in the way of them being friends only, partners in raising their child, was tearing him apart.

Since the night of the art exhibition, when he had told her about his parents and his first marriage, she was more open to him and in small subtle ways she was sucking him right into her world.

A world that he wanted to resist but was failing to.

When he had flown in from Madrid last Saturday he had joined her and her group of friends in a King's Road restaurant towards the end of their meal. She had excitedly shuffled along the booth to make space for him, including him in every conversation and insisting that he share her chocolate roulade.

Her friends, cautious at first, had accepted him enough to tease him about Charlotte's description of his impatience when it came to driving in London traffic.

She was texting him throughout the day, chatting freely in the evenings about how her day had gone. Asking him in turn about his day.

And when he needed to work late into the evening, she would bring him cups of coffee, playfully pinching her nose so as not to smell it.

But their attraction to one another, the chemistry between them, was acting like a barrier; it kept them wary of one another. A barrier that was needed. Because if they were intimate again, then their relationship would move to a level of complexity that neither might be able to control.

Seeing her so ill today, though, had shown him that he needed to balance this wariness and need to keep a distance between them with the support and care she obviously needed. Charlotte deserved to have a marriage, a relationship that was considerate and reassuring.

Downstairs, he found her out on the terrace, reading a pregnancy magazine, tucked beneath her new blanket.

Sitting beside her, he unrolled the plans, and pointed to the coach house to the rear of the garden. 'I've had plans drawn up for renovating the coach house into a two-bedroom mews.'

She stared at the plans and then at him. 'You want me to move into the coach house?'

What? Where had she got that idea?

'No. I—'

Jumping to her feet, she interrupted him. 'I'm taking the baby with me.'

She stepped back from him, clasped her forehead with her hand, heat exploding in her cheeks. 'It's a good idea. We should have thought about it before now.'

He stood. 'You're not moving out—don't be crazy. This is for your parents. I'm sure they'll want to spend a lot of time with you and the baby. I thought they'd like their own space when they do.'

'For my parents?'

'I know how much you worry about them.' He pointed towards the plans. 'I have specified that there is a lift to take account of their mobility in the future. Long-term they could move in permanently if it suited everyone.'

Charlotte stared at the plans again and then at him, agog.

Tears shone in her eyes.

His heart did a little kick-start.

She shook her head, still looking bewildered. 'Are you serious? Really?'

When he nodded yes she gave him a shaky smile. Her fingers slowly and tentatively touched against his arm. 'That's the nicest thing anyone has ever done for me.'

She came closer and he moved towards her without thought, helplessly lost to her smile, the cautious happiness shining in her eyes, and wrapped his arms around her waist, pulling her in close.

He inhaled the scent of her freshly washed hair, sweet and clean.

Into the material of his shirt, she whispered, 'Thank you.'

Her waist was tiny beneath his grasp.

He edged his hand down, his thumb stroking just above the swell of her hips. Hips that had danced beneath him the night they had made love.

They both pulled back, only an inch or two separating their heads, their noses angled, their mouths aligned.

Her breath settled on his skin.

He wanted to taste those lips, to feel the warmth and softness of her mouth. He wanted to kiss her neck, run his fingers along her spine, undress her.

He wanted her. He wanted to make love to his wife. To the woman carrying his child.

Her body pressed in against his.

Desire sliced through him.

This was madness.

He pulled back. Before this went too far. 'I need to do some work.'

Charlotte, dazed, her lips parted, nodded frantically. 'Of course. Thank you again. My mum and dad will be thrilled.' She considered him for a moment with hungry eyes. Attraction and desire swarmed between them.

She backed away towards the terrace sofa. And distractedly said, 'They…my parents…they really like you.'

His heart turned over.

He hadn't realised until now that he wanted them to like him, approve of him. 'Good.'

Charlotte gave him a dazed but happy smile.

And his heart sank.

What would her parents think of him if they knew the truth of their marriage, the truth of his past? Guilt clogged his throat.

'They'd like to get to know you even better. Will you come with me tomorrow to see them? We can tell them about the coach house together.'

It was the last thing he wanted to do. 'Wouldn't you prefer to go on your own?'

'I'd like you to be there.'

He stretched his shoulders against the tension in them and reached down to roll up the plans. He handed them to her. 'I'm working tomorrow.'

She folded her arms, refusing to take the plans from him. 'It's a Saturday.'

A silent standoff ensued, he holding out the plans to her, she defiantly ignoring them. With a sigh he said, 'Okay, I'll come.'

She took the plans from him. 'I'm glad.'

Cautiously she moved towards him.

Standing on her tippy toes, she gave him a tight hug.

And against his hair she whispered again, 'Thank you.'

It was not a hug driven by physical attraction but a tender, appreciative hug from a wife to a husband.

The type of hug he had been missing all of his life.

CHAPTER EIGHT

SOON AFTER MIDDAY on the following day, Charlotte heard the front door open and then close downstairs.

Lucien was back from the office.

She stepped into her fuchsia-pink kitten heels and looked in the mirror dubiously.

This morning, in a moment of madness on Regent's Strect, she had bought a new dress and heels that were nothing like the functional, conventional clothes she normally wore.

Given the soft, pretty design of the dress, she could only conclude that her pregnancy hormones were definitely creating a nesting instinct in her.

Downstairs she found him in the kitchen, standing at the kitchen island studying the coach house renovation plans with a cup of coffee in his hand, her bag of vanilla fudge to the side.

He didn't look as if he would be ready to leave the house in less than five minutes' time. She had told him this morning that they would need to leave by twelve-fifteen at the latest to make sure that they reached her parents' house in time for lunch.

Had he changed his mind?

Disappointed, she plucked her handbag off the

dark navy kitchen sofa and asked, 'Having second thoughts?'

He twisted around to her. And did a double take. 'Your hair—it's different.'

'I was at the hairdresser's this morning. She cut a few inches off.'

His gaze travelled down over her. 'And your dress—that's new too?'

Unable to handle how self-conscious she felt, she fingered her 1940s-style crepe dress with its box-pleat skirt. The dress had an off-white background with the tiniest prints of iconic lipsticks and perfume bottles produced during the 1940s.

Her kitten heels matched perfectly one of the lipstick colours.

Lucien placed his coffee cup down and propped himself against the edge of the island with a lazy sexiness. He was wearing navy chinos and a brilliant white polo shirt. Everything about him glowed. His white shirt, the glint in his eye, the bright, healthy caramel tone of his skin, his raw, street-fighter athleticism.

She clenched her hands together. Fighting the lick of desire whipping through her. The empty ache inside her.

'You look beautiful today.'

She gave a weak smile and said, 'Thank you.'

He smiled. And didn't say anything.

From outside she heard a lawnmower.

In the kitchen there was only a thick silence full of temptation.

Her gaze fell for a moment on the garden wall. Where she had lost her mind to him. Her heart pounding, needing to kill the torturous silence, she began to babble. 'I fell in love with the dress the moment I saw it. It's not my usual style but it's such a beautiful day, and my clothes aren't fitting me any more. I hope it's not too mumsy.'

She ran out of breath.

'Your dress is lovely, but I was talking about *you*, Charlotte. *You* are beautiful.'

His eyes bored into hers. Weak-kneed, she smiled. She needed to get out of here before she did something stupid. Like walk into his arms, kiss that gloriously smiling but yet menacing mouth, run her hands under his polo shirt to the warmth and strength of his chest beneath.

Shuffling her heavy handbag to her other hand, she brought them back to how their conversation had started. 'So, have you changed your mind?'

He gave her an amused smile and began to roll up the plans. 'About the coach house? No. I just wanted to double-check the lighting plan.'

'I meant about visiting my parents.'

He laid the plans down on the counter. 'You want me there, so I'll come.'

'But you're not happy about it.'

His mouth tightened. 'I don't like lying to them.'

She nodded and looked out to the garden.
Pleached lime trees ran the length of the boundary walls of the garden, low lines of box hedging
edging the paths, both giving the garden a formal,
elegant structure, which was softened by glorious
planting of large clusters of lupins and hollyhocks.
In a few years' time their baby would be toddling
through that beautiful garden, sometimes to continue on to the coach house to visit her grandparents.

*I will not hurt my parents. Why should they
carry the burden of my mistakes?*

She turned back to him. 'I see it as protecting
them. What good would it serve to tell them the
truth? Now can we go? We're going to be late.'

He didn't move when she took a few steps towards the hall.

But then his expression softened and his gaze
wandered over her again, lingering for the longest
while on her stomach.

A wicked glint grew in his eyes. 'We're going
to have a very handsome son, you know.'

Relieved that his good humour had returned,
she began to walk towards the hallway again. 'A
very pretty daughter, you mean.'

Lucien followed her into the marble-floored
hallway and said, 'A daughter hopefully as pretty
as you.'

He moved in front of her and held open the front

door. His silver Aston Martin was parked on the kerb outside.

Thrown by his words, annoyed by how stupidly pleased they made her, how much she wanted to believe them, she paused on the top step and turned back to him. 'You don't need to use your chat-up lines with me. I'm your wife, remember?'

His jaw tensed ever so slightly. He checked his watch.

For a split second he hesitated.

And then in one swift move he pulled her back into the house and shut the door.

He backed her against the hallway wall.

'What are you doing? We're going to be late. My dad is a real stickler for time.'

One hand landed on the wall above her, trapping her.

He was standing way too close to her. Towering over her.

Shrewd green eyes challenged her.

He lowered his head and asked, 'Do you think that I've forgotten that you're my wife?'

She swallowed against the sexy drawl of his voice, against the chemistry thumping between them. 'No.'

He cocked his head and raised an eyebrow.

Desire tugged hard inside her.

'Do you think that I lie when I say you're beautiful?'

If she moved forward a few inches and rose up onto her tippy toes she would be able to lay her lips on that sharp, arrogant mouth and stop him asking all of these awkward questions. 'Maybe.'

He drew back a little. The heat was still beating between them but his mouth was an even harder, more alarming line of displeasure. 'Why do you doubt yourself?'

She gulped against the wild thumping of her heart, but managed to give him a haughty glare. 'I don't.'

He dropped his hand from the wall.

And touched his fingers along the inside of her arm. At first he skimmed beneath the cuff of her short sleeve before moving down the skin of her inner arm, torturous inch by torturous inch, toying with her. Light-headed, she fought against how badly her eyes wanted to close, trying not to let the groan of delicious desire in her throat escape. His fingers lingered at her wrist, drawing lazy circles over her artery. Could he feel her pulse throbbing there?

She should move away. But his dangerous eyes and even more dangerous body held her captive.

His eyes darkened.

Her heart dipped as he stared at her as though he was trying to look into her soul. 'At work you like to portray yourself as cool and logical, an ice queen. It's who I thought you were at first, but the reality is that you're *une tigresse*. A tigress who protects her family, who protects her heart.'

And I need to protect it from you.

She pressed hard against the wall behind her. Trying to ground herself. Lost in a world where nothing mattered more than to feel the weight of her husband on her again. 'Perhaps.'

His fingers threaded down to hers. 'Your ex was a fool to have lost you.'

But you would have been happy to let me go too.

Sobering, remembering the truth of their relationship, she fell away from him on weak legs, desperately trying to pull herself together. 'Can we go now? My dad likes to have his lunch at precisely one-thirty every day.'

He studied her for a moment before opening the front door.

Outside, he opened the passenger door of the car for her, and when she passed him to sit in the car, he held her arm and said quietly, 'Some day you're going to let me in and allow me to see what's really going on in that brain, in that heart of yours. Some day you're going to actually trust me.'

Unable to meet his eye, she looked out blankly as he drove much too quickly through Mayfair following the satnav instructions to head southeast towards her home village close to Maidstone in Kent.

Knowing that she could never tell him why she doubted herself so much. How diminished, dismissed, worthless she had felt when the man she had loved had looked at her with such confusion and impatience when she had been depressed. She couldn't tell him because she didn't want to remember that time. She didn't want him to think her weak. Anyway, why burden him with all of that? What purpose could it serve?

Charlotte's parents lived in a house that would have been old even when Shakespeare was a boy. Set down a narrow lane off the main street of the village, it had a cottage garden to the front and a long lawn to the rear with fruit trees at the rear boundary wall.

Inside the rooms were timber-beamed with several open fireplaces, and low doorways Lucien had to duck through while trying not to tread on their tiny 'Yorkie-poo', Billy.

Billy was now repeatedly ramming a soft toy into his ankle, waiting for him to play yet another game of tug-of-war, as he sat out on the terrace with Charlotte at the garden dining table, her dad in the process of pouring them both home-made lemonade.

Charlotte's mother Carol paused from carrying out platters of food to the table from the kitchen, having refused to allow either of them to help, and eyed Charlotte with obvious pleasure. 'It's so lovely to see you wearing such a pretty dress.'

Charlotte touched the dress and shrugged. Again uncomfortable and disbelieving of any compliments.

Her mother's gaze narrowed. 'You look tired, though. Are you sleeping well at night, darling?'

Charlotte glanced at him and then away. 'Mum! Honestly.'

For a few seconds Carol looked at her, perplexed, before flapping her hands, an embarrassed expression on her face. 'Oh…no, that's not… I meant are you not sleeping well because of the pregnancy.'

Charlotte gave her an incredulous look.

Carol backed away, clearly anxious to make a quick exit. 'I'll get the salads.'

Her father walked away too, muttering something about checking on the barbecue.

Charlotte gave Lucien a cheeky smile, amusement glittering in her eyes, and he laughed. She leaned into him, her arm touching his, her head dropping against his shoulder for a moment before she pulled away.

Something strong and beautiful pinged between them.

A connection.

Was this what it meant to be a married couple? The intimacy you shared from spending hours together, the easy ability to read one another with a single look, to tease each other without uttering a word?

Her mum and dad soon reappeared and they settled down to a lunch of barbecued salmon and salads.

Halfway through the lunch, after much talk and gossip on village happenings, the intricacies of which made office politics sound like a walk in the park, Charlotte lowered her cutlery and said to her parents, 'When you visited you would have seen a coach house at the bottom of Lucien's garden.'

He grimaced a little that she still referred to *their* house as *his* but, oblivious to this, Charlotte continued on, 'Lucien has had a terrific idea. He's drawn up plans to renovate the coach house so that when you visit you'll be able to stay there.'

Carol clapped her hands excitedly. 'Oh, that's a wonderful idea. But are you sure? We wouldn't want to be getting in your way. You're a newly married couple, after all.'

Beside him Charlotte groaned.

Amusement and guilt stirred simultaneously inside him. He pushed both down and addressed Carol with sincerity. 'Charlotte and I will welcome your support and company. I'm sure your grandson will also love to have his grandparents so close by.'

His child would only have one set of grandparents in his life and he would do everything to make sure this warm and loving couple were an integral part of his life. Even if at times their love and happiness for one another, for Charlotte, painfully reminded him of just how lacking his own parents were.

Would he ever be able to match the Aldridges' easy love and openness?

With tears in her eyes, Carol exclaimed, 'It's a boy!'

Charlotte darted him a dirty look. 'We don't know yet, Mum. We've decided not to find out until the birth but Lucien keeps insisting it's a boy. But I know it's a girl.'

Robert, who had remained silent up to this point, stood up and raised his wine glass. 'I think it's time for a toast. Carol and I are delighted to welcome you into the family, Lucien. I have to admit that at the start we were concerned that you were marrying too quickly...' he stopped and gave a little cough, reddening a little as he glanced towards Charlotte's stomach '...even given your circumstances, but we can see now that Charlotte was a lucky woman when she met you. You're an honourable and considerate man.' Robert's chin wobbled. 'What more could parents wish for their daughter?'

Lucien drew back in his chair, about to drown in his own guilt. 'I'm not sure—'

The rest of his sentence was lost as Charlotte

interrupted, 'You're right, Dad. Lucien is incredibly considerate. Every year he donates millions personally to charities that provide much-needed housing to vulnerable and homeless young adults.' She stopped and inhaled a deep breath. Her mum and dad looked at her, a little confused, clearly not following why she was telling them this right now.

But he wasn't fooled for a second.

She interrupted because she had been afraid that he was going to say something that would give away the true nature of their marriage. Her words were hollow.

But then she turned to him, her cheeks growing hot, an intensity and admiration in her eyes. 'And just this week he announced at work a new apprenticeship scheme that will be rolled out in Huet this year, which will provide a training scheme for hundreds of vulnerable teenagers.' She smiled at him. 'I'm so proud to be the wife of a man who has worked so hard to achieve what he has, often with little support and in difficult circumstances, and the fact that he's so determined to help others now.'

His heart turned over.

He stared at Charlotte.

He stared at his wife.

He had been alone for ever.

With no one believing in him.

And now he had her.

He took a gulp of his lemonade.

His heart in free fall.

Her cheeks flushed, Charlotte turned to him and smiled at him shyly.

He wanted to kiss her. Right then and there.

He wanted to push her away. Terrified about what she was doing to him.

He wanted to be her husband, in every sense. To have her heart and soul. To connect with her emotionally and physically. Sleep with her. Make love to her time and time again.

But those weren't thoughts he should be having with her parents staring at him. Sitting in their garden on a blue-skied summer's day, when life suddenly felt as if it was full of possibilities.

He shook his head, pretending to be amused, modest, laid-back about all she said. When in truth they were the most meaningful words anyone had ever said to him. Words that were terrifying and wonderful at the same time. 'Thank you for the compliments but I'm far from perfect.'

A sparkle lit up in Charlotte's eyes. With an exaggerated sigh she said to her parents, 'He's right, he does have his faults.'

In unison Carol and Robert said, 'Really?'

'He drives too quickly.'

Carol looked appalled. 'Oh, Lucien, you mustn't—especially with Lottie being pregnant. With her past problems we—'

Before Carol could finish her sentence, Charlotte interrupted, 'And he steals my fudge.'

Robert shook his head. 'That's not a good idea.'

Charlotte shot him a narrowed gaze. 'And he works way too hard.'

'Well, that's to be expected,' her dad conceded.

Confused, Lucien turned to Carol. 'What problems?'

A tense silence fell on the table. Carol, clearly flustered, glanced at Charlotte, reddened a little but then acted as though she didn't hear him. 'When are you going to go on your honeymoon?'

There was something they weren't telling him. He fixed his gaze on Charlotte but she suddenly had the need to grind a ridiculous amount of pepper onto her salmon. Carol and Robert managed to avoid his gaze too as they busied themselves with their meal. He bit down on the frustration that uncurled in him at being excluded and said in retaliation, 'We're going next Thursday to my villa in Sardinia, for a long weekend.'

Charlotte turned to him with her prosecutor stare. 'Darling, you didn't tell me.'

He gave his best smile to her parents. 'It was to be a surprise but I'm sure you don't mind me sharing it with your parents.'

She lifted her glass and muttered, 'I can't wait.'

He met her eye and spoke the truth. 'Me neither.'

CHAPTER NINE

EVEN WHEN ASLEEP Lucien held the alertness and rawness of a street-fighter ready for action.

Propped up on an elbow, Charlotte watched her sleeping husband.

This, the first morning of their so-called *honeymoon*, was the only time since they had married that she had woken to find him still asleep beside her.

Was there a significance to that?

All week she had given Lucien a hard time for announcing the break to Sardinia in front of her parents but he had retaliated by teasingly asking her why she was so reluctant to go away with him.

As if he was oblivious to the tension that was mounting between them all week at the idea of being alone together for four days in the sun, on their *honeymoon*, and all the connotations that that brought.

She had grumbled on Monday evening about her old swimwear not fitting any longer. His answer to that, his eyes blazing, a sexy grin on his mouth, had been that they could always go skinny-dipping.

Completely flustered at that suggestion, she had made an excuse to leave the house and ten minutes later had been ordering a milkshake in a diner in Soho.

She edged a little closer to him in the bed. Bristle lined his jawline and down the thick column of his neck. His mouth was a sharp horizontal line, as dangerous as any blade. The faint hint of a lone acne scar close to his left ear made her think of him as a teenager, fighting to make his way, to escape his past. What strength and resilience he must have had. Could she wish for a better man to be the father of her baby?

She should get up and explore. And stop ogling her husband. They had arrived late last night but even in the darkness she had been blown away by the sprawling six-bedroom single-storey property with its extensive grounds located close to the exclusive resort of Porto Cervo on Sardinia's northeastern Emerald Coast: Costa Smeralda.

She should get up and go for a walk on the golden sands of his private beach or perhaps go for a swim in the shimmering blue Mediterranean Sea, both visible through the open French doors from where she lay in the bed.

She should get up and keep her distance.

But instead she stared at him. Her husband. As usual sprawled over his half of the bed, limbs thrown in every direction. The sheet twisted around his body revealing the power and hard beauty of his golden chest. His nearest arm tossed behind his head, the muscles of his biceps taut and bulging.

'The light is killing me.' His voice groggy, he scrunched his eyelids even more firmly shut.

She threw herself down onto her pillow, hoping he hadn't realised she had been staring at him for the past ten minutes. Trying to sound as though she had just woken too, she said in a low voice, 'I can't imagine a nicer way to wake up—to this view and the sound of the sea.'

'We're shutting the blinds and doors tonight.'

'Oh, don't be such a spoilsport.'

He twisted his head to her and opened up an eye. 'Spoilsport?'

She tried not to smile, not to react to how he was now watching her with sexy mischievousness. 'You heard me.'

'You're the one who refused to go swimming last night.' His sleepy voice was sexy, adorable, toe-curlingly tempting.

'You woke me in the middle of the night!' The desire to move to him, to lay her head on his chest, feel his arms around her, be wrapped up in his warmth, was crushing.

A slow grin formed on that lethal mouth. 'Where's your sense of adventure?'

'I'm adventurous!'

'Really? How about you prove that?'

In one quick movement he was out of the bed

and staring down at her. 'First to the pool gets to decide if we swim…with or without clothes.'

He was joking. Wasn't he?

'No way!'

He smirked at her protest and sauntered to his dressing room.

She was adventurous.

She didn't need to prove it to him.

Who was she kidding? She lived life by the book. Maybe it was time to throw caution to the wind. And regain the light-hearted girl she once was.

She rushed into her dressing room; the bedroom suite had 'his and hers' dressing rooms with doors that led to a shared palatial bathroom.

She searched her suitcase for a bikini and shouted out to him, 'This isn't fair. I have two pieces to change into.'

He answered back in a drawl, 'I'll help you if you want.'

Time to get him back. 'That would be great. I'll need to tie up my hair—my elastic bands are in my wash bag in the bathroom. Would you mind getting me one?'

The crash of something falling came from the bathroom, followed by a low curse.

With fumbling fingers she tied her bikini top while making for the open terrace door.

Outside she rushed down the pale yellow stone path that led to the infinity pool, her feet brushing against the coarse ticklish grass of the manicured lawns bordering the path.

She glanced behind her.

Lucien, in short-legged navy swim trunks, watched her from the terrace. A menacing smile on his face. Like any predator, happy to toy with his prey before he went in for the kill.

She gave an involuntary but heartfelt yelp and walked more quickly.

Genuinely scared. Thrillingly so.

She held a hand to her bikini bottoms, her forearm resting on her swollen belly, the other hand resting on her top. Praying that her newly purchased bikini continued to preserve her modesty.

Goosebumps serrated her skin.

She prayed that she wasn't waddling but it was difficult to pull off a graceful walk when eighteen weeks pregnant.

Light, assured footsteps sounded behind her.

She gave another yelp and tried to lengthen her stride.

In a few steps she would be at the wide terrace surrounding the pool.

Another few steps after that and she would have the safety of the water. She was about to win.

But suddenly a muscular arm was about her waist, lifting her up, carrying her forward along the terrace and away from the direction of the pool.

They passed a row of sun loungers and then she

saw where he was taking her: a four-poster canopied double sunbed.

He gently placed her down onto the mattress so that they lay on their sides.

At first she giggled, but then she pushed him hard on the chest. 'I win.'

'Nope, I don't think so.'

'You manhandled me!' She eyed him evilly and tried to get up but his arm once again circled her waist.

'I think on this occasion that I win.'

His tone was sexy, dark, full of suggestion. She went to respond but the heat of his voice, the heat in his eyes, the heat of his hand on her back, stole all of her words away.

Their thighs were touching.

Only a few inches separated their chests.

A hunger for him stormed through her. So fierce, so intense, so pointless, she couldn't breathe.

His thighs moved forward. Pressing more firmly against hers.

Desire moved through her body like a cascade of falling dominos.

He angled his head closer to hers.

Beyond caring any more about hiding her attraction to him, she whispered, 'Can we get up? Because I can't handle this for much longer.'

He didn't answer but continued to hold her gaze.

His bright green gaze so devastating her heart looped and looped and looped in her chest.

His mouth hovered over hers.

Their breaths mingled.

And with deliberate, heartbreaking slowness his lips moved onto hers.

Soft, enquiring, tentative.

But when she gave a give-away moan, his kiss turned hot and seeking. Urgent. Turbulent.

Six weeks of denial of the chemistry between them exploding into an endless kiss of release, hunger, desperation.

His mouth was hard. Demanding. Taking.

She groaned against his mouth when his leg wrapped around hers, his torso cradling into her side. His hand moved over her ribs and skimmed her breasts.

And still his mouth was on hers.

She wrapped her arms around his neck.

Needing more.

Glorying in the feel of his hard, powerful, domineering body entwined with hers.

His hand moved down, over her hip bone.

Deep desire ached inside her.

She wanted him.

She had wanted him from the first moment she had ever seen him, walking towards her on the executive floor at work. His long stride, dangerous air, streetwise gaze, fascinating and intimidating.

An innate potent attraction she had never experienced before that had her trying to convince herself that she had imagined it.

Now his hand moved up and over her swollen belly.

The kiss lightened.

His hand no longer frantic but a light caress.

His mouth still on hers, he whispered, 'The baby.'

Her heart turned over.

This was the father of her child. She was carrying his baby inside her.

Her heart felt as if it were about to burst with the bond, the closeness she felt for him.

She wrapped her hands more firmly on his neck, tried to pull him back to her. Needing his mouth, needing his body, needing him.

But he jerked away.

Punch drunk, she stared at him, lost in a jumbled world of connection and desire.

He inhaled deeply and untangled his body from hers. 'We can't…you'll only end up hating me. There's too much at stake.'

She edged away from him. Sat on the corner of the sunbed. Light-headed with desire and disappointment. 'What do you mean I'll hate you?'

He stared at the pale yellow stone beneath his feet, his jaw tense. 'I'll never be the husband you need or deserve.'

Humiliation, frustration and fear combined into fury. 'Isn't that up to me to decide?'

He didn't answer but instead stood up and walked to the side of the pool.

She waited for him to dive in, but he turned away and walked back up the path to their bedroom. Not once looking back towards her.

She collapsed back onto the sunbed, tears of frustration and loneliness burning the backs of her eyes. She dragged the light blanket that sat at the bottom of the bed around herself. Feeling cold and silly lying there in her bikini.

He'd done the right thing.

But right now she hated him for it.

Hated him for persuading her into this lonely marriage.

Later that evening, Lucien inhaled a lungful of dread when he turned to see Charlotte make her way down the path from their bedroom, to the pool terrace where he was waiting for her.

She was wearing what must be more of her recent purchases: a short gold miniskirt, a loose spaghetti-strap cream silk top and gold sandals; her hair hung in loose waves down her back.

A troubled goddess.

Her gaze met his only fleetingly.

He couldn't bear this any longer.

How was he supposed to take her to dinner and pretend that this morning didn't happen?

How was he supposed to not give into the temptation of touching his lips to her already sun-kissed skin?

And later on, to lie in the same bed as her but not be able to draw her into him, to taste her, to make love to her?

All day they had avoided making eye contact. As they had shared lunch, spent the afternoon on his yacht moored out of Porto Cervo, tension had bounced between them.

He had wanted nothing in life as desperately as he had wanted to untie Charlotte's mouth-watering apple-green bikini this morning. To love her body again.

To lose himself in her warmth.

To have the soft swell of her body beneath his.

To hear her cries of contentment.

But how could they do any of this when they had a child to raise together?

They had at least twenty years ahead of them where they needed to be able to support each other and work together. Mixing the emotions and expectations of being lovers into that would jeopardise their ability to get along.

And anyway, if Charlotte knew the full truth of his past, she would realise that she couldn't trust him.

She needed to know that truth.

Damning shame twisted in his chest and he reluctantly gestured to the beach. 'Let's go for a walk before we leave for dinner. There's still enough light.'

Her mouth tightened and she pointed a foot towards him, her raspberry-painted toenails, her long toned legs almost undoing his resolve to go through with this conversation. 'These sandals weren't made for the beach. We can talk at the restaurant.'

'We need to talk in private.'

She studied him unhappily for a few seconds before sitting down on a lounger and whipping off her sandals.

He removed his own moccasins.

Down on the beach, they sank into the fine sand, the light lap of the sea the only sound.

He steeled himself, suddenly overheating despite the fading sun to the west. 'I haven't told you everything you should know about my first marriage.'

She slowed her pace, caution replacing her annoyance.

He tried to speak but the words tangled and stuck in his throat.

She was the first person he would tell this sorry, pathetic tale to.

She stopped and turned to face him, her hand shielding her stomach. 'Our marriage isn't conventional. I don't expect you to tell me everything. Our past can be our own business.'

'After this morning, you need to know. You *need* to know why we can't sleep together. I hate lies. Ever since I found my father in the act of betraying my mother I've abhorred dishonesty. And to my shame I've been dishonest with you.'

A light breeze caught her hair and it swirled around her. She gathered it together and twisted it into a rope. 'What do you mean?'

He needed to walk. He couldn't face her when telling her this. He turned away and she joined him to walk along the crescent-shaped beach.

'Towards the end of my first marriage, Gabrielle and I were constantly arguing. We both hated where we lived, sharing with so many others, the noise, the rodents, how run-down and unsafe the property was. I wanted to move to Paris for better opportunities. Gabrielle refused to. We were growing apart but neither of us wanted to face that fact. Until I arrived home one night and found her semi-naked in the kitchen with another man who shared the apartment. She eventually admitted that it hadn't been the first time they were together.'

She pulled him to a stop, her hand resting on his arm. 'That's horrific.'

He moved away. Not able to bear her touch. Knowing how much she would hate him when he told her everything. 'It tore me apart. Despite our problems, I thought she was the one person I could rely on. Trust. I wanted to hurt her, as much as she had hurt me. I went out and got drunk.' He looked into Charlotte's troubled and horrified eyes and admitted his darkest secret, saying the words, fighting the crunching tightness in his chest. 'And then I slept with her friend.'

Charlotte gasped. Backed away, stumbling in the sand. 'You betrayed her, with her friend.'

He looked away from her crestfallen expression, the hurt in her eyes.

'Oh, Lucien, how could you?'

He winced at the pain in her voice but forced himself to look back and face her disappointment in him. 'I'm not going to try to defend myself.'

Her expression hardened. 'I should hope not. Did you tell your ex what had happened?'

'The next day.'

She planted both hands on her hips and lifted her chin. Fury pouring from her every pore. 'What you did was selfish, stupid and immature. How could you? I know Gabrielle betrayed you first. But what you did was no better.'

At that she walked away from him, furiously striding down the beach, her body rigid with anger.

He stayed put. Knowing there was no point in following her. Knowing there was nothing else to be said. She now knew what type of person he really was. A man who betrayed his wife. A man a thousand times more contemptible than her ex who had broken her heart.

For well over ten minutes she stared out at the sea at the far end of the beach.

And as the minutes ticked by his self-disgust turned to dread.

What if she wanted nothing to do with him after this?

Had he just compromised his child's future because of his past, because he couldn't handle his feelings for Charlotte?

What had he done?

Her eyes closed, Charlotte lifted her chin, desperate to ease the tight tension in her neck, the onshore breeze lifting her hair away from her shoulders.

He had betrayed his wife.

And she had no idea how to respond.

She flung her eyes open.

He still stood where she had left him, further up the beach.

Over black trousers he was wearing a light soft-knit black sweater. His dark clothing adding to his intensity, dignity, pride even when admitting something so terrible.

She had always said he was a heartbreaker. A manipulating charmer. Unreliable and selfish. And if he had told her this before they had married, before she had got to know him, she would have walked away.

She stalked back towards him, needing to lash out.

Still not quite sure what she was going to say.

She had to think of the baby.

But she also had to think of herself. Of her heart.

She came to a halt before him and the words tumbled out furiously. 'I hate what you did. You're a better man than that. Why did you do something so horrible, so stupid?'

He winced but held her gaze.

The self-recrimination in his eyes blunted her anger.

She inhaled a shaky breath, her heart dipping to see the tight lines of distress at the corners of his eyes. She bit her lip against the uncertainty, the broken dreams twisting inside her, but mostly in compassion for Lucien's pain. 'But I know what it's like to hurt, to be afraid. We don't always act well when we're scared.' She had isolated herself from others when depressed, pushing them away. How many people had she inadvertently hurt? 'You were young. Young and stupid. What you did was wrong, really wrong, but we've all done things we regret.'

He shook his head and said bitterly, 'I'm sure you never did anything quite as stupid as I did.' He stopped and his expression tightened further. 'I'm particularly sorry that it only acts as a reminder of how Dan betrayed you.'

She closed her eyes at the memory of how Dan and Angie had stared at one another in the pub garden after they had broken away from their kiss. Their love for one another puncturing endless holes in her already depression-ravaged heart. Now she looked at Lucien and said, 'Knowing what you did does hurt. But I have done things I too regret. I regret how I was with Dan towards the end of our relationship...things were tense and sad between us.'

She paused and drew in a breath into her unbearably tight chest. She had pushed Dan away, not wanting to contaminate him with her unhappiness. While at the same time unfairly willing him not to allow her to push him away, wanting him to believe in her, fight for her. 'It doesn't excuse what Dan and Angie did, but I do know that things are never black and white in life, and that relationships are complex and messy.'

Lucien reached forward and repositioned the thin strap of her top that had fallen down her shoulder. His touch as gentle, as intimate as his voice when he asked, 'What went wrong between you?'

Her heart pinched. A shiver darted up her spine. She should tell him about the depression.

But she couldn't.

She gestured back up the beach. 'I'm getting cold. I need to go to the villa for my wrap.'

They walked back up the beach, a wide gap separating them. She needed to give him an explanation as to why she pushed Dan away. To explain at least part of her regrets. 'Back then, Dan and I were growing apart. We just weren't able to talk like we used to, university was coming to an end, we had careers to think about, I wanted to move to London, Dan wanted to move to Manchester for work.'

'Were you still in love with him?'

Emotion the size of a bowling ball landed on her chest. 'Yes.'

At the bottom of the steps leading back up to the terrace he stopped and looked at her soberly, his jaw working. 'Are you still in love with him?'

She looked her husband in the eye and answered, 'No.'

But I am with you. Stupidly.

She shrugged and continued, 'We all make mistakes. It's only human. It's not making them again…that's the important part.'

At the top of the steps Lucien stamped his bare feet on the flagstones to remove the sand clinging to his soles. 'But do we ever change? What if those mistakes happen because they are an integral part of you? What if it's genetic? And you do it again.'

'What are you saying?'

'I grew up with selfish parents who were irresponsible, who sabotaged every relationship they ever had. What if I'm the same?'

'Are you saying that you might sabotage our relationship?'

His eyes held hers with a steady strength full of pride but a keen awareness of his past and the hurt he had caused. 'I'll do everything in my power not to. But with my background how can I swear to you that I won't hurt you at some point in the future? And the worst part is I know you'll never rightly trust me after hearing this.'

'Maybe I will.'

He shook his head. 'No, you won't.'

She picked up her sandals and stabbed them towards him, angry to hear the stubborn defiance in his voice. ' I won't pretend that I'm not really disappointed that you betrayed Gabrielle, but I will trust you and do you know why? Because I now understand that, with your background, it would have been so much easier for you not to marry me. But you still went ahead for the sake of our baby. You turned your life around when you were so young, when everything was going against you, and that takes immense strength and courage. You did all of that alone, without support. It's about time you had support, someone who believes in you.'

She swallowed hard and stepped towards him.

She touched the soft wool of his sweater, her heart thundering. 'I'd like to be that person. If you'll let me.'

His hand moved down and covered hers. He pulled her into him, his arms wrapping around her waist. 'Why?'

She spoke her words into the warmth of his throat. 'Because you're the father of my child. My husband.'

Because I'm in love with you.

His hands tightened around her waist. His lips brushed against her ear. In a voice full of dark emotion he breathed out, 'I want to be your husband in the fullest meaning of that word. I want to make love to you.'

'You do?'

He answered with a soft groan. But then he held her gaze with serious burning green eyes. 'I'll never want to hurt you.'

He meant it, for now. But she knew better than anyone that life could change you, change how you thought you would act and behave.

She smiled at him shyly, her heart thumping with need to connect with her husband. Whatever the future might bring for them.

On the nearest sun lounger, he wiped her feet clean of sand. His movements gentle and tender.

A precursor to the night ahead.

CHAPTER TEN

THE FOLLOWING MORNING a warm body cradled Charlotte and a rainfall of soft kisses dropped down along the side of her neck and over her bare shoulders.

Her eyes closed. She wanted to stay in this dreamlike state for ever, and she murmured little moans of appreciation when his hand moved down over her hips, along the length of her thigh and back up to caress her bottom.

His mouth nibbled on her ear.

She giggled and tried to move away, but he pulled her in closer, wrapping her in the cocoon of his heat and tight, taut body.

She had almost fallen back to sleep when he whispered against her cheek, 'Come and watch the sunrise with me.'

Drowsily she twisted around to him.

The corners of his mouth were crinkled; happiness, mischievousness, lingering want shone brightly in his eyes.

A long luxurious feeling moved through her: the feeling of being sated, contented, worn out.

She stretched lazily. 'I'm too tired.'

Playfully he ran kisses over her cheeks and down her throat. She giggled and tried to push him away. Which only encouraged him to run his kisses further down until his mouth was playing havoc once again with her breasts.

She moaned and her body lifted, desperate to press against him.

He lifted his head, triumphant, and asked, 'Still too tired?' He didn't wait for her answer but instead climbed out of the bed.

He disappeared into his dressing room but soon re-emerged dressed in jeans and a tee shirt. His feet bare.

He plucked his sweater from the evening before off the floor and brought it to her. 'Wear this.'

Sitting up, she reluctantly pulled on the gorgeously soft sweater, her sleepy haze intensifying as she inhaled his lingering scent on the wool fibres, all while trying to protest that it was too early, too dark outside. She wanted him back in bed with her. Holding her. Distracting her from her thoughts. Thoughts that had her panicking about just how deeply she was in love with him.

Last night he had made love to her so slowly, so tenderly, so intimately that she had completely lost her heart to him.

Now he listened to her protests with amusement, clearly not prepared to give in to her.

She shuffled back in the bed, pulling his sweater down to cover the tops of her thighs, her back against the headboard. And pulled an ace from her sleeve. 'I'm pregnant…cut me some slack here. I've barely slept all night.'

He wasn't falling for it. He flashed her an evil grin and swooped her into his arms.

He carried her through the open terrace door and followed the lit path down to the pool terrace.

She tried to pull her sweater down over her bottom where it had ridden up but his fingers, clasping her at the top of her thigh, flicked her hand away.

She groaned as those fingers then teasingly caressed the sensitive skin at the top of her thighs. She wriggled but he only tightened his grip. And in retaliation she nibbled the skin just below his hammering heart.

He cursed lowly.

And when he dropped her onto the double sunbed, he loomed over her and said, 'I think we have unfinished business here, don't you?'

Later, wrapped in each other's arms, they watched the sun, cautiously at first, but then in a fiery bold blaze, rise up in the east. And she pushed away all of the fears for the future that ebbed and flowed in her brain like the sea below them, knowing the only way she would cope was by not overthinking this situation. Yes, he was with her only because she was pregnant with his child. But maybe that was enough. Maybe his affection and friendship would suffice instead of love.

A week later, Charlotte locked the coach-house door that led out into the main garden and paused to dust herself down.

The builders had begun work on Monday and, five days in, they had demolished all of the internal structure that needed removing, insulated the inside and had begun to build new partition walls.

Lucien had left for meetings in Brussels Wednesday morning.

Two nights without him and she felt completely lost.

As much as she hated to admit it, she was in deep. Deeper than she wanted to be. But she was so consumed by him, so hungry to be in his presence, so distracted by him that she couldn't think rationally.

The pink and white tea roses and peonies now blooming in the garden glistened under the evening sun. It had rained earlier. London was being hit by short and fierce thunderstorms, and the air was filled with a mixture of rose blossom and damp earth.

A movement on the terrace had her start.

And then she smiled.

He was home early.

He wasn't due home until tomorrow afternoon in time for a charity ball they were attending in Somerset House.

She stood still.

And drank him in. Her heart flapping. Her entire body trembling.

Her husband. Dressed in a dark navy suit, his purple and silver tie loosened, the top button undone.

With his hard body, solid neck, sharp jawline and cleft chin, he was still a street-fighter. But one with honour and integrity.

He cocked his head to the side.

Waiting for her to go to him.

About to go, she wavered. Needing to stay in control.

He pulled off his tie.

Threw his jacket onto a nearby chair.

And sauntered towards her.

Night after night for the past week, they had made love time and time again, waking each other during the night with a never-ending hunger to connect again. And during the day they sneaked out of work at lunchtime and spent the hour in bed, Lucien poker faced when they returned to HQ, Charlotte blushing at the speculative glances of the receptionists.

He came closer.

Dark, dangerous, all-consuming, his expression one of absolute desire.

He towered over her. She was unable to breathe against the fire in his eyes.

A single finger touched against her stomach.

She shivered. Closed her eyes with a sigh.

Both hands clasped her face, his long fingers threading through her hair.

She opened her eyes and mouth at the same time.

And she moaned hard and long when his mouth claimed hers.

He unbuttoned her dress in the garden.

Removed it in the kitchen.

Made love to her on the thick, inviting wool of the living-room rug.

Not a single word passed between them.

The following evening, butterflies dancing in her belly, Charlotte ran out into the hallway from the kitchen when she heard Lucien rush down the stairs.

'We're going to be so late. Did you have to go into work on a Saturday? You…' The rest of her admonishment for him being so late home faded as she drank him in.

Standing a few steps up on the stairs, he was unbearably handsome in his bespoke tuxedo.

Her cruel, sexy assassin…with a heart full of honour and kindness.

Her king amongst men.

But he wasn't quite perfect.

She dashed up the stairs towards him. 'You can't go to the ball with wet hair.'

'It'll dry on the way there.'

'It's not even a ten-minute journey away. Come on, I'll dry it for you.'

In their bedroom she pulled out her dressing table stool and gestured for him to sit.

He did so reluctantly.

The moment she touched his hair, she knew that it was a bad idea.

Now they were definitely going to be late.

Her fingers ran through his hair, the tips skimming the hard contours of his scalp. The ever restless ache inside her for him igniting.

And he stared at her in the reflection of the mirror. Stared hard. Stared with the look of a man who liked what he saw.

Hungry. Compelling. Formidable.

Overwhelmed, she twisted to the side, so that the reflection would only show her back. And she bowed her head so that he wouldn't be able to catch her eye. Embarrassed by how much she wanted him, at how weak, how defenceless and vulnerable she was around him.

Male power oozed from him.

Her fingers danced through his dark brown hair. Above his right ear, her fingers touched against his scar. She had felt it on the first night they had been together but hadn't learnt how he had acquired it until he had told her of his childhood. It represented so much about this strong man who had defied what life had thrown at him.

He turned his head a tad towards her. His gaze shifting up, devouring her.

She glanced away, heat and an intense intimacy for her husband firing through her.

She longed to move her hand down further, to feel the strength of his neck, touch her lips to his skin, and inhale his earthy, leathery scent.

But they were already late.

She switched off the hairdryer.

Needing to break the tension, she joked, 'I don't suppose a milkshake will be on the menu tonight? My cravings for one are off the scale at the moment. It must be the humidity.'

Instead of answering, he reached forward and placed one hand on her waist, anchoring her to the spot while the other gently landed on her ever increasingly rounded stomach.

Her legs wobbled beneath her.

He pulled her towards him and down onto his lap.

At the same eye level now, his green gaze engulfed her. 'You're truly beautiful tonight.'

She swallowed and smiled. Incapable of speaking.

The yearning ache inside her for him widening.

His hand moved up over the loose jersey folds of her full-length gown, caressing her legs beneath.

She shivered.

And he groaned before his mouth lightly touched against hers.

She twisted in his lap. Aching for him to touch all of her.

He deepened his kiss and she moaned when his hand moved up over the satin sash at her waist to the floral lace of the gown top, his fingers lightly teasing her heavy breasts, before they moved to the deep V at the back of the dress.

She squirmed into his lap and deepened their kiss when his fingers ran along her exposed spine.

They were *definitely* going to be late.

His hand moved down to her stomach. Their kiss lightened. Became tender. A soul-destroying connection to this man, her husband, the father of her child slammed into her.

They pulled away from one another.

And she could see in his eyes that he felt it too.

She loved him.

It was reckless and stupid.

But she loved him.

She was looking heartbreak in the eye and couldn't do anything about it.

She wanted to cuddle into him. Have him hold

her for ever. She wanted him to make crazy, passionate love to her. She wanted to get up and never turn back, walk away now while she could.

And then she gasped and looked down in astonishment to where Lucien's hand lay on her belly.

A second ripple travelled through her stomach. 'Was that the baby?' he asked softly.

Her hand flew to her mouth. Tears popped up in her eyes. 'Yes…yes…oh, Lucien, our baby moved.'

He let out a shaky breath. Gave her the most incredible smile. And pulled her into his lap even more tightly. Tucked her head against his collarbone. One hand tightly holding her to him, the other hand resting on her stomach, protecting their child.

Charlotte pulled back her tears. Knowing she needed to be strong for this baby. She needed to remain logical and realistic in what she could expect from him. He would be a good, perhaps even brilliant father. But as his wife she could never expect or demand his unconditional love.

But now, for five minutes even, she wanted to be held in the safety of his arms and forget reality.

Four hours later Lucien walked down the steps from the cloakroom to the courtyard of Somerset House, his heart tightening once again when he spotted Charlotte standing watching the iconic fountain show that had water jets hidden in the cobblestones, shooting synchronised powerful spurts of water upwards.

He juggled from one hand to the other her heavily beaded red silk wrap he had gone inside to retrieve.

His attraction, his affection…his love for her was spiralling out of control.

He was besotted by her.

And it made him feel ridiculous. All night, instead of being focused and concentrating on his conversations with some of the City's big hitters, first out on the river terrace overlooking the Thames where the drinks reception had been held and later during dinner in Somerset House's vast neoclassical courtyard, he had been distracted by the sight of Charlotte in her full-length red gown. Hating to see her chatting with her male legal acquaintances, the way she flicked back her loose hair, smiled at them openly, a crazy urge to snarl and claim her as his wiping away all reason.

He loved her.

But he wasn't sure if he would ever be able to tell her. In telling her, he could destroy what they had. He could frighten her away. He could open emotional floodgates neither of them could contain.

He couldn't lose her.

He couldn't lose this baby.

He couldn't risk telling her he loved her because

he couldn't bear the thought of her not loving him
back. He couldn't bear the thought of failing her
in the future. He couldn't bear the thought of ever
losing her. Of being rejected. Again.

Now, despite the noise of the swing band playing on the stage and the chatter of the other guests,
she turned to him as he approached, as though
she sensed his presence without looking. Across
the crowd for a brief second he caught her worried expression. But then she smiled at him shyly.

They were leaving the ball early. Dancing together on the crowded dance floor, beneath the
night sky of the courtyard, the historic buildings
surrounding them bathed in a pale blue light, he
had whispered into her ear that he wanted to take
her home and make love to her. She had looked
at him, her eyes heavy with desire, her cheeks
flushed, lips slightly parted, and nodded.

And a sudden need to be truly intimate with his
wife had rocked him.

An intimacy that was more than just about making love.

He wanted to be closer to her emotionally. To
really understand her.

But he didn't know how to get fully inside her
head.

Was that even possible?

Was he being unrealistic? Surely the physical attraction and burgeoning friendship between them

should be enough. But yet…but yet a kernel of dissatisfaction, of something not being quite right, gnawed away inside him.

He placed her wrap around her shoulders and planted a light kiss on her forehead.

Took her hand in his.

And together they walked towards the archway that led out onto the Strand, where his driver was waiting for them.

He pushed away all doubts and focused on the here and now by asking, 'Any more movement?'

She shook her head with a wry smile, her hand clasping his more tightly. 'Not since you last asked me ten minutes ago.'

He gave her a guilty smile.

Laughing, she added, 'I promise to tell you when she does kick again.'

He should work tomorrow. He had to fly to South Africa on Monday. The quarterly results for Huet were positive but the next quarter's projections were worrying him. South America's growth was falling way behind target. Despite all of that he heard himself say, 'Let's go shopping for the nursery tomorrow. We can have brunch in my club and then look at the specialist nursery furniture stores we saw on King's Road the night we had dinner with your friends.'

Last week they had agreed to convert the bedroom across the corridor from theirs into a nursery. With windows overlooking the rear garden, the room would be perfect.

Despite the warmth of the night, he felt her shiver. She pulled her hand free of his and drew her wrap in closer around her shoulders. 'I'd prefer to wait until nearer my due date.'

Her voice echoed sharply against the neoclassical columns and stonework of the archway. He drew her to a stop with a sense of foreboding. 'Are you worried?'

'No, but I suppose I'm just being cautious… I don't want to tempt fate.'

He wasn't following. Charlotte liked order and logic. He didn't have her down as someone who was superstitious. 'Tempt fate?'

'What if we buy things and something goes wrong.'

The worry in her eyes had him step towards her. 'Nothing will go wrong.'

She backed away and glanced out towards his waiting car. 'Let's wait at least until after the scan next week.'

He followed her, and pulled her to a stop. 'Why do you think something might go wrong? Is there something you're not telling me?'

'No.' She worried her lip and said in a rush, 'It's just that you never know, do you?' Her wildly blinking eyes clung to his, before she looked down to the ground. 'If you can't make the scan on Thursday, it's okay.'

Where did that come from? She knew he was determined to go to the scan. 'Don't you want me there?'

Charlotte looked away from the sharp intelligence in Lucien's eyes. 'No...no, of course I want you there. I just know how busy you are.'

Guilt rushed through her. Twisting her stomach into a tight knot. The truth was that she didn't want him there.

At her twelve-week appointment she had discussed at length her past history of depression with her obstetrician consultant.

But what if the consultant, whom she was also scheduled to meet, said something at the appointment?

Logic kept telling her that it wouldn't happen.

She could always ring and ask for it not to be mentioned in front of her husband...but even the thought of that made her cringe with guilt and embarrassment.

She needed to stop panicking.

She attempted a bright smile and said, 'You're cutting your trip short to come back for the appointment. It just seems excessive. I can bring my mum if you would prefer for someone else to be there.'

He eyed her dubiously. 'I'll be there. I told you that I would.' His hand moved under her elbow and he led her towards his car.

It was close to midnight and the streets and pavements of Trafalgar Square and Piccadilly were alive with Saturday-night revellers. They spent the journey home in silence. Lucien's steadfast gaze out towards the passing streets. She had insulted him by suggesting he might not want to go to the scan.

Once home and in the kitchen, he was as attentive as ever, asking if she wanted something to drink, but there was a distance between them. A distance she had created.

A jolt of realisation slammed into her. She shuddered and for a moment grew light-headed.

How would I cope if he ever shut me out of his life? Just with this silence I feel like I'm being scissored in two.

Unable to bear the tension between them, she said, 'I'm sorry.'

Those streetwise, uncompromising eyes held hers. 'I will be at the scan on Thursday. I *want* to be there. You don't have to test me on it, by giving me a way out.'

Was that what he thought?

'I wasn't…' She stopped at his questioning frown, having no alternative explanation to give to him. 'I'm sorry.' She gave him a small smile. 'I hate it when you're annoyed.'

The faintest hint of a sparkle of amusement grew in his eyes. It freed something in her and she added, 'You're pretty scary when you're annoyed, you know.'

For the longest while he stared at her. And then he walked to stand before her on the far side of the kitchen island. His hand cradled her cheek and then ran down the length of her hair, skimming the side of her breast. 'Scary good or scary bad?'

With a gulp she admitted, 'Don't-dare-mess-with-this-sexy-tough-guy scary.'

At that he delivered her a sinfully dazzling smile. 'I'll take sexy scary.'

And she smiled at him goofily.

His eyebrow lifted and he stepped closer. 'Take your dress off.'

Her pulse went into overdrive at his growl. Heating up by at least twenty degrees, she jumped away.

There was an evil glint in his eye.

'Seriously?'

His expression darkened. 'I think you should prove just how sorry you really are.'

He was calling her bluff again. A deep vulnerability stirred in her, all of her old insecurities threatening. But the fire blazing in his eyes torched all those vulnerabilities. She wanted to undress for her husband.

She reached around and pulled down her zip. Dropped one lace shoulder and then the other.

Lowered the dress to her waist.

He groaned when his eyes lighted on her red lace bra.

She eased the dress over her bump and the material dropped to the floor.

He ran a hand along his stubbled jawline, muttering, 'I guess you are sorry.'

His eyes skimmed over her. Over her breasts, her stomach, her matching red panties. Down to her red stiletto heels and back up again. His gaze burning into her.

Please let him come to me. Wrap me in his arms. Wrap me in his warmth. Wrap me in his softly murmured words when he makes love to me.

He moved in front of her. Cupped a cheek into the warmth of his hand. And smiled with a sexy badness before he turned away and walked out into the hallway and up the stairs.

Bewildered, she stood there unable to move for what felt like a lifetime.

But then she reached down and yanked up her dress.

But before she made it out of the kitchen, to head upstairs to tell him precisely what she thought of his mean little trick, he was back. With a pair of her maternity jeans, a cosy sweater and trainers.

He handed them to her. 'I know a great diner in Camden that does the best milkshakes ever.'

She'd prefer him…but a milkshake sounded

pretty good too. Especially with him at her side. She pulled on her jeans and then her sweater, happiness bubbling through her. 'You're a genius, Lucien Duval, and I think I'm falling in love with you!'

Lucien's smile faded.

Panicked by what she'd said, panicked by his surprised gaze, panicked by the intensity of her feelings for this man who was her husband of convenience, she added, 'I'm warning you, though, the diner better not be closed when we get there. Or you'll be way down on my list of favourite people.'

She rushed to the door, cringing. And was relieved when he opened the door and gave her a laid-back smile. 'I called ahead earlier…they are staying open especially for you.'

She breathed in a sigh of relief that he hadn't taken her words seriously.

And then breathed out a sigh of regret that he hadn't done so. But why would he think she might love him when the only reason they were together was for their baby's sake?

Tuesday 12th July, 8:32 p.m.

Missing me?

Sorry, who's this? C

Funny. I miss you.

Bet you're out in a club with clients right now. C

A Cape Town restaurant, in fact.

Pretty girls there? C

I haven't noticed. Send me a photo of yourself.

I'm not that sort of girl! C

I meant fully dressed…unless you'd prefer otherwise.

Wow, Charlotte. Crossed eyes suit you.

Bet you're regretting marrying me now. C

Meeting you was the best thing that ever happened to me.

Wednesday 13th July, 6:43 p.m.

Meeting delayed here. Won't get back tonight. But will be back in time to collect you for the scan appointment at twelve tomorrow.

I'll have the sonograms to show you if you don't. C

I'll be there. I'll call you later. I'm about to make a presentation to the clients.

I'm meeting Tameka and Jill later. I'll speak to you tomorrow. C

I miss you.

You too. C

Only now do I realise what was missing from my life.

A cross-eyed pedantic legal head? C

Family and belonging.

I'm glad. C

CHAPTER ELEVEN

ON THURSDAY MORNING, Charlotte sat alone in the Ultrasound waiting room at Claremont Hospital waiting to be called for her scan. Thanks to a French air traffic controllers' strike Lucien's plane had landed into City Airport late and he was likely to miss the appointment.

He had sounded exasperated when he had rung her earlier at work to tell her that he had organised for a company car to take her to the appointment. And she, like a traitor, had breathed out a sigh of relief that there would be no danger of her history with depression being revealed to him.

What kind of wife am I to be glad that my husband won't be able to attend our baby's scan? Am I that selfish that I'll put my panic, my fears above his happiness?

Needing a distraction from her guilt and the nervous energy bubbling in her stomach at the prospect of the scan and the ever-present worry that a problem with the baby might be detected, she went and rifled through a pile of magazines left on a console table in the corner of the room next to the water fountain.

She searched through the tall column of magazines not taking them in, too overwhelmed by the guilty ache twisting and twisting and twisting inside her.

Towards the end of the tower of magazines, she came to a stop. And let out a disbelieving sigh as she yanked out a glossy magazine.

Below the magazine's main front cover of the royal family attending church in Sandringham on Christmas Day last year, there was a photo of Lucien attending a West End premiere. His date that night had been one of the UK's top female track athletes, who was leaning into him, a wide ecstatic smile on her face.

Despite Lucien's moody scowl at the camera, the body language between them was so relaxed, so intimate, it was obvious they were close... lovers close.

She tossed the magazine away. And shut her eyes. Jealousy heating her stomach. With a groan she sank her head into her hands.

She was in love with Lucien and it terrified her. She didn't know where she stood with him. How he really felt towards her. *Family and belonging.* That was what his text last night had said had been missing from his life. But what did he mean by that? Was he only growing close to her because of their child? Was this still only a *business marriage*...that had veered into the confusing depths of lovemaking?

He had opened up to her about his past. That

spoke volumes, didn't it? But maybe he saw her as a partner, a friend, someone he was fond of rather than in love with.

'Is everything okay?'

She yelped at the sound of his voice.

Standing at the waiting-room door, suit jacket in his hand, and despite needing to shave and his shirt being a little wrinkled, Lucien was as big and formidable and sexy as ever.

Adrenaline zipped through her.

She went to speak. But her mouth refused to co-operate. Pleasure, relief at seeing him, the dizzying realisation that in fact she did want him here, all competing with a rush of fear that he might now find out about her depression from someone other than her.

How would he react? Would he slowly but inevitably distance himself as Dan had? Would he think of her as weak? Would he be wary of her because her depression might one day return? Would he find her less attractive? Could he even use the knowledge of her depression against her somehow?

He walked to her and his hands came to a rest on her shoulders, concern and anxiety shining in his eyes. '*Qu'est-ce que tu as?* What's the matter? Is there something wrong with the baby?'

She shook her head.

He bent down to look her in the eye. He gave her a small concerned smile. Willing her to speak.

She swallowed against how much she wanted him to hold her, against how her heart was banging wildly against her chest in pleasure to see him.

She dragged in a deep breath, a sense of unreality washing over her. Was she really going to tell him? She hadn't spoken about her depression with anyone other than her medical team in such a long time. Her stomach lurched violently and suddenly she was shivering. She had to force the words out. 'I have something I need to tell you.'

Lucien paled.

Horrified, she said in a rush, 'It's nothing to do with the baby. I haven't been seen yet. The couple before me only went in five minutes ago.'

He led her to the wooden chairs set into the semi-circle of a large bow window and sat beside her, his body tense, his expression a mixture of concern and confusion.

She gripped her hands against the churning in her stomach.

'There's something you should know about my past medical history.' She paused and inhaled a shaky breath, cringing at how hot her cheeks felt.

His expression grew grave. Oh, God, was she doing the right thing in telling him? He had married her because she was going to be the mother of his child. He hadn't signed up to be burdened with this.

Her knees were jiggling like crazy but she couldn't control them.

Just say the words. Why are you making such a big deal over this?

'In my final year of university I had depression.'

He looked at her blankly. And then his eyes grew wide. He drew back in the chair. 'Depression?'

Hating to see his shock, she nodded and stood, backing away from him until her back was pressed against the wall on the opposite side of the room.

For the longest while he just stared at her. As though he wasn't able to process her words.

After an excruciating few minutes he stood and took a step towards her. A sadness flooded his eyes. He shook his head as though perplexed. 'Why didn't you tell me about this before?' The sadness in his eyes was nothing in comparison to the hurt in his voice.

Guilt squeezed her heart painfully. But the panic rolling through her was even more intense. She didn't want to talk about this any more. 'It was ages ago and I've been well for such a long time. I'm not on medication now. It's not a big deal.'

He looked at her as though mystified. And then he twisted away and walked to the other end of the room. And back towards her. And away again.

This time he didn't turn back but stood staring at a noticeboard filled with leaflets on antenatal care at the opposite end of the room.

She wanted everything to go back to how it had been. 'It's great that you got here in time.'

He didn't respond. Didn't turn around.

She moved closer, clutched her hands together and said, 'I missed you.'

Now he did turn. But it was as if he didn't hear her. His expression dark, shrewd, wary. 'Why are you telling me about this now?'

Her mind went blank. Fresh panic unfurled within her. There was a weariness, a distance to him that was frightening her.

'Why, Charlotte?'

She moved back from him. The urge to run away overwhelming. 'I wanted you to hear about it from me rather than someone at the hospital.'

His jaw tightened. 'If I hadn't insisted on coming to the appointments would you have told me?'

She felt all hot and clammy. Her heart was beating way too fast. She closed her eyes, her stomach churning, and said, 'I'm not sure.'

When she opened her eyes again, he was staring at her with disbelief.

She began to babble. 'I'm better now... I was on medication for a few years, but I no longer am. I practise yoga and mindfulness every day—I take care of myself.'

A horrible silence settled on the room.

She wanted to get away from him.

She wanted him to offer her comfort. She wanted him to see the terror inside her at the prospect of having to tell him about her depression. How she couldn't bear to have to relive all of that hurt and pain and fear again. She wanted him to recognise how vulnerable, how fragile, how weak she felt right now.

But instead he looked at her as though he didn't know her any more.

It was to this hideous silence that the sonographer swung open the door, cheerfully calling out Charlotte's name with a warm smile of welcome.

In the darkened room, Lucien stared at the images of his baby on the screen, a thick wad of emotion stuck in his chest, making it difficult to breathe.

He could make out his nose, his hand, his foot.

He should feel joy.

But instead he felt numb.

For a few crazy weeks he had thought he had found a family. A woman he trusted and loved. But she hadn't trusted him.

Had she always intended to keep her depression from him? Or was it when he had told her about sleeping with Gabrielle's friend that she had decided not to?

From the corner of his eye he saw her look towards him.

The wad of emotion in his chest hardened.

He was never going to get away from his past. She was never going to trust him.

He should have kept their marriage strictly business. Not revealed so much about himself.

He stared at his baby on the monitor screen.

For the first time in his life he had thought he had found a connection, a closeness, a safe harbour with Charlotte but it had all been wishful thinking on his part.

For years he had numbed himself to the need for closeness, for care. Needing to erect a barrier against the pain of parents who resented him and then a failed marriage.

The bitter taste of sadness and shame grabbed his throat. Charlotte did not accept him. Value him enough to share something so significant.

He stared at the monitor, the numbness spreading through his body like a virus.

An hour later, back home, Charlotte stood on the terrace and listened to the thud of music coming from an open window of the coach house. The builders' radio. The music was drowned every now and again by the sound of heavy banging.

The music and building noise were oddly reassuring after the tight silence of her trip home with Lucien after the hospital appointments. Both the sonographer and her consultant, whom they'd met after the scan, were pleased with the baby's development.

And she had forced herself to ask her consultant to explain to Lucien the consequences of her past mental-health history. Lucien had listened intently and asked his questions in a matter-of-fact manner.

Lucien was now upstairs changing. They were both going to head back into work once he was showered and changed. When they had got home he had made her tea and asked if she was okay, in a formal, stiff, distant manner.

They were like strangers once again.

A light movement fluttered in her stomach. She placed her hand there and stared down, trying not to let the tears at the backs of her eyes escape.

How was it possible to love someone you hadn't yet met so much?

To feel such love even when your heart was beginning to crumble?

Saturday afternoon Charlotte went to the front door and for a moment placed her hand on the wood panel. Steadying herself against the nervous energy that was coursing through her body.

The doorbell rang again.

She forced herself to smile and opened the door to her parents.

Her mum swept towards her and dragged her into a quick hug before bustling past her, heading in the direction of the kitchen. Her dad stepped into the hallway and lowered the umbrella they had been sheltering under.

His kind blue eyes ran over her. 'How are you, Lottie?'

A lump lodged in her throat.

Please let nothing happen to him. Please let him know his grandchild for years and years.

'It's great to see you, Dad.'

His slow hug almost undid her. The heavy weight of his arms on her back, the reassuring familiar scent of his damp tweed jacket. The comfort it brought bringing home just how alone she felt in this house, in her marriage.

She glanced up the stairs as they went to the kitchen. Lucien knew her parents were visiting this afternoon. Her stomach knotted. Would he be as remote with them as he was with her?

Since Thursday, he was at home more than he had ever been before. They were talking but it was perfunctory. Stilted conversations on how their day had been. How she was feeling. It felt as if he thought he had to be at home rather than wanting to be there.

In bed at night she craved his touch. Wished

with all of her heart that he would pull her into his arms and hold her. Tell her that he was there for her. More than anything she wanted his comfort, to feel safe with him again.

They were living in the same house, but it was as if he were absent. He was there, but out of her reach.

And with each passing day the fear inside her that he had never really been there for her grew. The heart-shattering confirmation that this marriage was never anything more for him than a means for raising their child together. And growing close to her had been nothing more than a sensible approach to making their marriage tolerable.

Another summer storm had hit London, bringing brief relief from the heatwave that had sat over the city for weeks now. Rain lashed against the kitchen windows.

Her mum stood at the kitchen island unpacking a heavy carrier bag filled with dented old tin Christmas biscuit boxes that brought back memories of school bake sales. With a smile of satisfaction her mum opened each tin. 'Fruit scones, apple squares and, especially for Lucien, the coffee and walnut cake he likes so much.'

Charlotte opened a kitchen cupboard to get some plates, the sense of being a visitor in this house overtaking her again. The sense of being an imposter in her own life. It felt wrong to be entertaining her parents in his house. It felt wrong to be pretending to her parents that her marriage was a happy one.

'Is Lucien home?' her dad asked, taking a seat at the kitchen table she had earlier set for their afternoon tea.

'He's working at the moment but he hopes to be able to get down to see you at some point, in between his conference calls.'

They poured tea and ate the scones while her mum recounted in detail what had happened at the village fete that had taken place the previous weekend. Charlotte sipped her tea but struggled to eat.

As usual her mum noticed. 'Are you okay, Lottie? You're...' she paused and her eyes flickered anxiously over her face, taking in the dark circles under her eyes that Charlotte hadn't been able to erase even with the aid of concealer '...you're looking tired.'

Before she could answer, her parents' attention was diverted by the sound of Lucien's footsteps out in the hallway. For a split second when he came in the door she saw displeasure in his eyes when his gaze moved over their little tea party. Did he resent them all being in his house?

Her heart stumbled.

Please don't drag my parents into this.

But then he smiled affably towards her parents

and allowed her mum to hug him and he shook her dad's hand.

He didn't move to sit with them so, attempting a relaxed voice, she asked, 'Will you join us?'

His gaze moved over her and then settled on the rain-soaked windows. 'I need to get back to work,' he said, looking back to her mum and dad, 'but I thought you might like a tour of the coach house— if you don't mind going back out into the rain.'

Charlotte felt relief and disappointment at the same time. Relief that he was welcoming to her parents, relief that he still envisaged them visiting and staying here in the future. But disappointment that not once since he had come downstairs had he looked her in the eye.

Her mum answered first. 'That would be lovely… and a little rain never hurt anyone. But first you must show us the scan pictures from Thursday.'

Charlotte got up and retrieved them from her bag on the kitchen sofa. The set of pictures from her twelve-week scan sat proudly next to Lucien's computer upstairs. But neither of them had thought of these scan pictures since Thursday. Their poor baby had been forgotten in the standoff between them.

She brought the pictures back to the table and gave one to each of her parents. She glanced quickly at Lucien. In a quiet voice she said, 'You must take one for your office.'

For a moment something softened in his expression. But then he looked away.

Her mum oohed and aahed and asked, 'Did you find out whether it's a girl or boy?'

'No, as I've said before we want to wait until the birth to find out,' Charlotte answered, pushing away the small voice in her head asking if there would be a *'we'* by then.

Then her father, who had been carefully studying the sonogram, said, 'The details are incredible. I can see a foot and hand. After everything you went through that time you were unwell I never...' Her dad came to a stop and glanced at Lucien in alarm.

His expression unreadable, Lucien said quietly, 'Charlotte told me about her depression during the week.'

Both her mum and dad visibly winced at the word depression. They still preferred to call it *the time she was unwell.*

'That's a relief. Lottie should have told you from the start. But she's always been closed about the whole thing,' her mum said.

Charlotte shot her mum a warning glance. 'Mum.'

'But you have, Lottie. You would never talk to your dad and me about it. And it's not something that you should keep from your husband.'

At this point her dad cleared his throat loudly. 'I

think we should take that visit of the coach house now, don't you, Lucien?' He stood without waiting for Lucien to respond.

Lucien stood but tension whipped off him. His jaw tightened before he glanced down at her. 'Do you want to come with us?'

She shook her head, her throat tightening to see a brief flicker of disappointment in his eyes before they once again became guarded. 'I'll stay and tidy up.'

When they had gone, she stood at the kitchen island, midway in clearing up, holding a tin box in her hands, watching Lucien guide her parents down through the garden, slowing his pace for them, holding an umbrella in both hands to protect them both from the rain. And the ache of loneliness in her deepened…she wanted so badly to be able to turn to him for comfort and care, to know that he was there for her.

How long more could she keep up this exhausting pretence of a happy marriage?

When they eventually returned from the coach house, her parents speaking enthusiastically about the space, her dad especially animated over the plumbing and bathroom fixtures, Lucien held back and watched her silently.

Seeing afresh his distance, the constantly closed way he observed her now, when her dad, who was always nervous of driving in London, said that they should be leaving soon, she blurted out without thinking, 'I've been thinking that I will take annual leave next week.'

All three stared at her.

'You're right, Mum, I am feeling tired at the moment. The heat here in London is stifling.' She glanced briefly towards Lucien but it hurt too much so she turned to her parents. 'Lucien is leaving early tomorrow morning for Toronto and will be away all week so would it be okay if I come home with you now?'

CHAPTER TWELVE

SATURDAY EVENING LUCIEN stared at his semi-packed suitcase and realised he hated it. Hated everything it symbolised. Before he had married he had loved to travel. Loved the anticipation of the new and exciting. But the sad fact of it all was that travel was only another way of him trying to escape the loneliness of his life.

Living with Charlotte, coming home to her each night, chatting over dinner, making love to her, talking afterwards in the dark, he had felt truly connected to another person for the first time. And it had given him a sense of acceptance and security that had quietened the agitation, the unhappiness that had rattled inside him all of his life.

Until the scan appointment on Thursday.

'It's not something that you should keep from your husband.'

For crying out loud, even her mother understood that.

He slammed the suitcase lid shut and stormed downstairs.

Restless, hating the silence in the house, he went into the lounge on the first floor and switched on the television. He flicked it off after five minutes, unable to concentrate.

On the library shelves surrounding the television, next to his collection of biographies, were the books Charlotte had brought with her when she moved in. He ran a finger along the spines of the mostly pregnancy books and romance novels.

For someone who professed she didn't believe in love she certainly read enough about it.

I think I'm falling in love with you.

Had she meant it when she had said that the night of the Somerset ball? Or had she been joking? He had seen her shock at having said those words and, not knowing how to react himself, had chosen not to ask her to elaborate on what she meant. He hadn't wanted to ruin what they had, their delicate burgeoning relationship, by pushing her. But now, all he could think about was how could she possibly say those words with any sincerity but yet keep something so personal and intimate from him?

From outside came the loud squeal of a child's laughter.

He went to the window and saw a family playing out in the park at the centre of the square. The mum and little girl giggling as the father tried to retrieve an errant Frisbee from dense and thorny rose bushes.

He turned away and went down to the kitchen.

There he opened the fridge door, knowing he should eat something.

His eyes were drawn to a bottle of Sauvignon Blanc on the wine rack at the bottom of the fridge.

It was years since he had last had a drink.

Would there be any harm in starting again? Just one glass?

His stomach churned.

And he slammed the fridge door shut.

She had gone home.

But this was supposed to be her home.

He grabbed his keys and wallet from the console table in the hallway. He had to get out of this house now. The silence was unbearable.

On the way to the River Bourne, Charlotte passed through the kissing gate to cross Carpenters Lane and heard the whack of a cricket bat from the village cricket green. As a child, she had spent her summers at the river, swimming and hanging out with her friends. Those friends, just like her, had all left the village for careers and marriages. Would she be the first to return?

It was four days since she had last seen Lucien. He texted and called every day but their conversations were stilted and remote.

What was she going to do?

She missed him. She loved him. But could she stay in a marriage that left her feeling so insecure and vulnerable?

Could she stay married to a man who didn't love her enough?

She skirted along the side of Stewarts Field, the late afternoon sun warming her, bees and butterflies fluttering and dipping around the vibrant yellow rapeseed crop.

She passed through another kissing gate and followed the bare earth path that wound its way down to the river, tall hedges thick with blackberry bushes on either side. She used to come here every September to pick plump blackberries with her friends after school.

Would she be bringing her little girl here too?

She drew in a ragged breath. Would she be a single mum then? Would it be only the two of them, with Lucien visiting at weekends? Hot pain grabbed her heart. How would she cope with having him in her life but yet having him so distant, so disconnected from her? To not feel his arms around her again, his breath on her skin, his whispers of affection.

At the river she walked alongside the riverbank until she came to the point where it had collapsed down into a gentle slope of soft earth that allowed access to a deep pool of water. She dropped her rucksack onto the grass and placed her picnic blanket beneath the dappled shade of an ash tree.

She lay down and closed her eyes. Tired to the marrow of her bones.

She had hoped that in staying with her parents she would finally manage to get some sleep in her childhood bed, away from the torture of having to lie in Lucien's bed and all of the memories that existed there. But she lay awake most nights, twisting and turning, thinking about him. Wondering where he was, what he was doing at that precise time. At times angry that he had shut down on her. And at other times resigned to it with a sadness that chewed ferociously at her heart. He had married her because of their child; he had never said that he would love her.

A thought flickered through her mind. She tried to catch it but it flickered away. He hadn't said he'd love her…but…

Charlotte shot up to a sitting position on the blanket.

Their wedding vows.

Her heart thumping in her chest, she remembered the words.

I promise to be always open and honest. And, whatever may come, promise to provide you with comfort and support through life's joy and sorrow.

She sank her head into her hands.

How had they come to fail one another so badly?

Early Friday morning Lucien wearily opened the front door.

He had packed five days' worth of meetings

into four, needing to get home. Knowing he had to go to Charlotte at her parents' house and talk with her.

He had destroyed one marriage.

He couldn't do the same with this one. Not when there was a child involved.

But first he needed to shower and change.

And drink a litre of espresso to fight his jet lag.

He left his suitcase in the hallway but brought his carry-on bag upstairs and into the spare bedroom across from theirs. From his carry-on he pulled out a cross-eyed tortoise he had found in the window of a toy store on Queen Street yesterday when travelling to a construction site meeting.

His first present for his son. He placed it on the double bed of the room, fixing the little blue bow tie the tortoise was wearing.

They had planned for this room to be the nursery. But that was no longer a certainty. Just like their marriage.

He flinched as a hollowing-out pain twisted his heart.

Their marriage couldn't continue like this. How could they raise a child in the tense, awkward atmosphere that was between them now? An atmosphere that possibly would only disintegrate further and further into blame and bitterness.

There was no way his child was going to be

brought up in a household like that. History was *not* going to be repeated.

He turned to leave but then spotted a small snow-white Babygro on the room's chest of drawers.

When had that appeared?

It hadn't been there on Saturday night when he had sat in here after he had come home from his club at two in the morning, having taken part in a late-night poker game with other members in preference over the silence awaiting him at home.

He picked up the tiny piece of soft fabric.

And swallowed against the tightness at the back of his eyes.

He shook himself.

He placed the Babygro back where he had found it and inhaled a deep breath.

Please let me be right on this...please let this mean that she has come home.

He opened the door to their bedroom. His heart tripped over. Charlotte was asleep...lying on his side of the bed.

He came closer and stood watching her chest rise and fall beneath the soft pink lace of her nightdress. Only a sheet covered her, the beautiful swell of her bump clearly visible beneath the light cotton. How he missed placing his hand there, the surge of emotion, the intimacy, the connection that knocked him for six every time he touched her and their baby beneath her taut, warm skin.

He wanted to climb in beside her. Hold her.

Would she turn to him? Or curl herself into the tight ball of limbs and silence she had recently adopted. Shutting him out, silently saying, *I don't trust you. I don't need you.*

He didn't want to wake her but they needed to talk. Before his jet lag worsened and he was incapable of any coherent thought. Reluctantly he crouched down before her and called her name.

Her drowsy eyes opened. Groggily she smiled at him. Her lips a gentle curve of contentment.

For a few glorious seconds hope surged through him.

But then the drowsiness cleared and she shot up in the bed and retreated away from him, pulling the sheet up around her. 'I thought you were in Toronto until Saturday.'

He tried to ignore the pain of her withdrawal, the wary caution in her eyes. 'I need a quick shower but I'll make us breakfast after. We need to talk.'

She nodded with a sad acceptance and shuffled further against the pillows at her back, readjusting the sheet.

He went into the bathroom and switched on the shower. His whole body and soul aching for her. Needing to be close to her again. But panic was churning in his stomach. Would she ever fully let him know her? Or was his past always going to haunt him?

He found her in the garden after he had showered and dressed.

Wearing a grey jersey tank dress, she was sitting on the terrace drinking her usual first-thing mug of decaf tea.

He settled for tea too and sat at the garden table alongside her.

The tips of her shoulders were red. He bit back the urge to tell her off for not wearing sunscreen and asked instead, 'I thought you were staying with your parents for the week.'

She dropped her mug to the table. Touched her hand to her forehead. For a few seconds blocking him out. Then she looked at him with sad, sad, sad eyes. And gave an even sadder smile filled with sorrow. 'I was out walking yesterday and I thought about our vows. Do you remember what we said?'

Confused, he shrugged while trying to recall the exact words.

'I promise to create and protect a family and home that's full of love, understanding, respect and honour.' Charlotte paused and her gaze met his before she continued, 'I promise to be always open and honest.' She went to speak again, but couldn't get past, 'And whatever may come…'

He clenched his hands around the wooden slats of his seat, guilt and regret clogging his throat. And finished off the words he had said on their wedding day. 'I promise to provide you with comfort and support through life's joy and sorrow.'

Charlotte forced herself to remain looking at Lucien. Even though it tore her apart to hear him say those words again. Tore her apart to have such tension, so many unsaid words between them.

Despite his shower and fresh clothes he still looked exhausted. The hard lines on his face deeper, the shadows beneath his eyes adding to the bewildered pain in his eyes.

'Why didn't you tell me about your depression?' he asked quietly.

I promise to be always open and honest.

She had broken those vows. Despite the dread and fear crawling along her skin, the embarrassed heat on her cheeks, she met his gaze and answered, 'We barely knew each other. I...' She closed her eyes, unable to continue.

'But we did get to know one another.' With an expression of sad bewilderedness, he added, 'At least I thought we did.'

She clenched her hands. 'I didn't want to burden you... I was worried about how you would react.'

Lucien recoiled in his chair and then came forward again. 'What do you mean, how I would react?' The softness of his tone was gone and was now replaced by angry disbelief. 'I'm your husband, for crying out loud. I thought you trusted me... I told you everything about my past. Everything. Every single pathetic thing. I opened up to you. And you kept your depression from me. How can we function as a couple if you don't trust me enough to really let me into your thoughts, into your past?'

She knew he was right, but the pain and loneliness in her, the fear that she wanted so much more from this marriage than he did, weren't about to be silenced so she cried out, 'The only reason you married me was for the baby. You weren't signing up to be burdened with my mental-health history. You heard my consultant—the risk of me developing postnatal depression is higher because of it, I didn't want to burden you with that possibility.'

He closed his eyes for a moment, his jaw tightening. Her heart dropped down to her feet. Was he about to say out loud what she already knew: that he couldn't handle, support, be there for her should her depression ever return?

Please. Please. Don't.

She jumped up and fled while muttering, 'I'll go and make us breakfast.'

In the kitchen she yanked open the fridge and pulled out random items with trembling hands.

She yelped when she turned around to find him standing only feet away from her. His expression sombre. 'If your depression did recur we would deal with it, as a couple, as a family.'

She swallowed hard. So desperately wanting to believe him. But knowing that in reality he was only saying it because he wanted them to stay together for the sake of their child. 'I don't expect you to. I'd understand it if you wanted to walk away.'

'Of course I would be there for you. You're my wife. I told you when I asked you to marry me that I would take my vows seriously. I won't walk away from you. You mean too much to me.' His jaw tightened and a raw vulnerability entered his eyes before he continued, 'Is it because of my past... my parents' marriage, how I destroyed my first marriage, that you don't trust me?'

'No! Of course not. Not telling you...it had nothing to do with your past.'

His cynical stare told her he didn't believe her.

She had to be honest with him. Her legs weak, an emptiness opening up inside her, she propped herself against the fridge door and admitted her deepest fears. 'When I told Dan about my depression, he wasn't there for me, not really, at first he tried to be, but the reality of having a girlfriend with depression soon took its toll on him and he resented it. I was terrified that you would be the same. That you'd see me as a burden. Think less of me.'

He stepped back from her. 'I thought you knew me… How could you think that I would see you, my wife, as a burden?'

His voice, his expression, were filled with pain.

Matching her own heart churning confusion and fear. 'But since I've told you about the depression you've been so watchful, so detached. It has felt as though you're worried about me…but only because I'm carrying your baby.' Unable to stop, the hurt and vulnerability of the past week bubbling in her chest, she added, 'I've been so lonely without you.'

Lucien sank his head into his hands, tiredly rubbing his face. When he looked back, his tortured eyes held hers. 'I'm sorry.' He twisted away and walked to the kitchen island where he placed his hands on the counter, and stretched his back. When he eventually turned back to her, he said, 'I couldn't understand why you hadn't told me. It ripped me apart. I wanted you to trust me enough to tell me. I felt like a failure, knowing you couldn't trust me. A failure because my wife couldn't rely on me, didn't need me the way I needed her. But how could you trust or rely on me? Knowing the destructive environment I grew up in. Knowing how it has messed with my head as my first marriage demonstrated.'

He was so wrong.

A surge of protectiveness for him steamed through her. 'No. I'm not having that. You're a strong and honourable man. Why on earth do you think I fell in love with you?'

'You're in love with me?'

Her heart somersaulted and fell over at the disbelief in his voice. 'Of course I am.'

'You said you loved me on the night of the Somerset House ball but I didn't know if you were serious.' He stopped and looked at her, bewildered. 'But how can you love a person you don't trust?'

She stepped back, punched by his sadness, by his words. 'I do trust you. I love you.'

He gave her a resigned look full of regret. 'But if you don't let me know you fully how can we survive as a couple?'

Tears of hope and confusion and terror stung at the backs of her eyes. She bit her lip, squeezed her hands, her nails digging into her palms, and asked the hardest question of her entire life. 'But do you want us to survive?'

Lucien's heart crumbled at her softly spoken question. She loved him. But he needed more. He needed to fully know his wife. 'Yes, I want us to survive, but you have to let me know you.'

'For the sake of our baby?'

Was that what she thought?

He wanted to move to her, take her into his arms and comfort her as he should have done days ago.

I promise to provide you with comfort and support through life's joy and sorrow.

He had said those words. And had meant them.

But at the first hurdle in their marriage he had not honoured them.

Shame washed over him. But he pushed it away. Now had to be about Charlotte, not his guilt. 'I want our marriage to survive because I want *you* in my life. *Je veux être avec toi pour toujours.* I want to be with you for ever. But to do so, I need to know you.' He stopped and tried to fight the inadequacy swelling up inside at voicing his fears, for showing weakness. But he needed her to know *him* too. 'I need to feel safe with you and while you continue to guard yourself from me I will never feel that you trust me.' A plug of shame clogged his throat but he forced himself to continue. 'I grew up knowing I wasn't wanted by my parents. I can't handle a marriage where I'm not truly wanted, accepted, needed. Where I feel insecure.'

She came towards him, the anguish in her eyes matched by that in her voice. 'I do want you. I do love you.'

A thousand emotions choked him, leaving him struggling for air. Did she love him enough to let him in, to share her most intimate thoughts?

'Tell me about the depression.'

Charlotte looked at him with terrified eyes before grabbing a box of eggs and studying it uncertainly. Eventually she said, 'I was twenty-two. Apart from the usual dramas of falling for the wrong guys and exam worries, I was sailing through life.' She stopped and shrugged, her expression haunted. 'But in my final year, with exams looming and the pressure to get a first-class honours degree, I started to feel overwhelmed, unable to cope. I kept telling myself that I needed to be stronger, but I got more and more exhausted. I couldn't concentrate. Everything started to feel grey. I was constantly anxious. I had panic attacks. Life...life felt so hard. I had no interest in anything. Especially the future.'

Without warning she turned away and pulled open the pan drawer beneath the hob. 'You must be hungry. Would you like an omelette?'

When he didn't answer she turned to him, a frying pan in her hand.

He went to her and took the pan from her. 'Speak to me, Charlotte. Tell me about that year.'

She backed away until she was pressed against the hob. Disquiet in her eyes. For a moment she hesitated but then said impatiently, 'I didn't tell anyone for ages, especially my parents. I hated failing them. I hated being so weak.'

She grabbed the frying pan out of his hands

and said, 'I'll make you a mushroom and ham omelette.'

He wanted to take the pan back off her. But could see that she needed to be busy. She cracked three eggs into a jug and whisked them furiously before peeling and chopping mushrooms like a woman possessed.

Eventually she said, her voice angry and sad all at once, 'My parents were so upset when my GP eventually diagnosed depression that I knew I couldn't really talk to them about it. I felt so guilty. I didn't want to be a burden to them. So I pretended that I was okay.'

'But you weren't?'

'No. I was so, so sad.' Her face crumpled into a mask of distress but after a few seconds she inhaled a shaky breath and continued, 'I did tell Dan and Angie. At first they were supportive and understanding, but after a few weeks I could tell that they were getting impatient with me. They would change the subject if I spoke about how I felt. Or tell me that I needed to try to see the positives in my life. Which used to drive me crazy.' She threw her hands up irritably. 'If only I could have. If only it was that simple. And as the weeks and months passed Dan and I grew further and further apart. We met less and less often, and when we did it was awkward and we struggled to even talk.'

She turned back to the counter and clicked the gas ring of the hob on. And switched it off again. Her back to him, she said, 'All I wanted was for Dan to hold me and tell me everything would be okay. But he didn't. I hated him seeing me so ill. I hated how awful I looked. And then I found out about him and Angie.' She turned to him with tears in her eyes. For a brief second she held his gaze before she bowed her head and said in a quiet voice choked with hurt, 'When I found out about their affair I felt so useless, so hopeless, so worthless. I had lost too much weight and looked ten years older. I felt so ill and tired.'

Sharp thorns stubbed his heart to see her pain. No longer able to stay away from her, he went and placed a hand on her arm. The other reaching up to cup her face. Slowly and reluctantly she lifted her head. 'No wonder you doubt just how beautiful you are.'

A single tear dropped down along her cheek. She scrunched her eyes shut. 'The loneliness was the worst. I had no one to turn to. No one to offer me comfort. I was all alone...and I was scared of reaching out.'

No wonder she had kept it from him. 'And you still are.'

She opened her eyes and her fingers touched his hand that was cupping her cheek. He held his breath at the relief in her eyes. The connection, the intimacy that had been missing between them for much too long surged back. 'I decided the only way for me to cope was to be tough and not get hurt in a relationship again, to only focus on what I could control: my career, minding myself by being insular. I wanted to forget the past and focus on the future.'

He stepped even closer to her and said, 'Your future is with me now.'

'Is it?' Her question was asked with such trepidation and wonder and disbelief he found it difficult to breathe.

He ran his hand down over her hair. Time and time again. Wanting to touch her, soothe her, care for her. 'Of course it is.'

Her eyes wide, her cheeks flushed, she whispered, 'Why?'

'Because I love you. I want you in my life. I want to care and comfort you.'

'Even knowing about my depression?'

'There's no shame or weakness to having had depression. I don't think any less of you for it. I love you regardless. You said before that you wanted to support me. Well, I want to support you too.'

He smiled at the hope that was beginning to shine in her eyes. 'Your depression is only a small part of who you are. I love so much about you. I love you in the morning when you're sleepy and cling to me.'

He swung her around so that he was now leaning against the kitchen counter. He pulled her in against him, her baby bump nestling against his hip. 'I love you during the day when you're smart and bright and feisty at work. I love you in the evenings when I come home to you, come home to your happiness and teasing and gorgeous smile. I love you when you make me dinner with such enthusiasm, each meal making me feel more loved than any words could do.' She smiled at that. His heart tripped over.

He pulled her into him so that her cheek was resting on his chest. Into her hair he whispered, 'I love you in the nights when I can make love to you, when I can kiss your soft skin, when I can lose myself in you, when I feel complete for the first time in my life.'

Slowly and reluctantly Charlotte pulled herself out of the embrace she would happily stay in for the rest of her life and backed away. 'Can I have five minutes to get my head together?'

A flicker of apprehension crossed his expression.

Quickly she explained, 'I vowed to you that I would be open and honest with you. And I'm trying to be…but there's more I want to say. Words to explain how I feel for you. I want to get those words right.'

A smile lifted his lips gloriously upwards. 'But you're the *Verbal Assassin*.'

Happiness rolled through her. 'Yes and look what you've reduced me to—a jabbering wreck!'

Out in the garden she paced the decking.

He loved her. He loved her. He loved her!

He accepted her depression. She had seen it in the kind, understanding sincerity of his gaze.

He wanted her. Not just because she was carrying his baby. He wanted *her*.

Her husband loved *her*.

And I love him with every fibre of my being. I love him with all my soul.

Back inside the kitchen, Lucien was waiting for her, propped against the kitchen island. Looking nervous. She loved him even more seeing how edgy he was…how he waited for her to speak as though it was the most important thing in the world to him.

It was time she opened her heart to him. Completely. 'You say you really want to know me?'

At his encouraging nod she took a deep breath. 'Well, here goes—I fancied you the first time I saw you but thought you were a player. So I used to tell my colleagues who thought you were *"hot"* that they needed to have their heads examined. And then one cold March night you simply smiled at me and I lost my heart to you. That night we slept together was so special, so tender, I wanted more but knew I couldn't. And when I found out about my pregnancy I didn't want to marry you because I was terrified I'd fall in love with you while you'd have no feelings for me other than I being the mother of your child. But over the past few months you have showed yourself to be fair, full of integrity, a man who wants family and love. I have so much respect for everything you have achieved, for how generous and supportive you are to others... I just refused to believe that you would be the same with me. But now I can see how wrong I was.'

Lucien came towards her, his large body looming above her, sexily, protectively. Green brilliant eyes, assured and confident, held hers and he said, 'I saw you on my second day at Huet, at ten in the morning to be precise. I was heading to the boardroom and you passed along the corridor.' His voice dipped even further into a low sexy whisper. 'You were wearing a navy pencil skirt, a white blouse with gold buttons and navy heels.'

She shivered when his fingertips ran down the length of her arm. 'I think I fell in love with you right then and there. Even though you almost froze me to the spot with the icy stare you threw in my direction. I tried to convince myself I was crazy. I have never dated employees.'

His hip edged towards hers. She inhaled him, and grew even dizzier. He continued, 'But the night we made love, I couldn't stay away from you. And after we made love, deep down inside me I knew I was never going to let you go. But I didn't know how to get beyond my past and fear of messing up a relationship again.'

His hand reached down to her stomach and with a smile he said, 'But Robbie decided to make an appearance before I had worked out how to get you into my life permanently.'

She laid her hand on his. Her heart soaring. 'Robbie?'

'After your dad.'

She blinked away the tears. It proved a little more difficult to dislodge the lump blocking her throat. 'Will I make you that omelette?'

His eyes twinkled. 'Nope.'

She blushed at the suggestive smile on his lips and muttered, 'You're looking a little tired. Maybe you should lie down.'

His mouth dipped to her ear. 'I was going to suggest the same to you... I did wake you early on your day off, after all.'

A tremor ran through her body at his low whisper, and how he was now nibbling the lobe of her ear, a hand moving up to skim at the sensitive side of her breasts. 'I had hoped to spend the day in bed,' he whispered before drawing back, those brilliant green eyes, full of love, consuming her.

'In fact, we're spending the entire weekend there. We've a lot of catching up to do.'

And then he kissed her.

A kiss full of intimacy and closeness and connection.

A dizzying kiss so full of love and tenderness that she wobbled against him, light-headed and weak-kneed.

With an affectionate laugh he lifted her into his arms.

And for three days they closed off the rest of the world.

Loving and cherishing each other for every precious second.

EPILOGUE

EARLY CHRISTMAS MORNING Charlotte paused at the downstairs lounge door, her heart skipping a beat.

Inside, the only light came from the golden tree lights, shimmering like a thousand wishes on the Christmas tree. And in a chair next to the tree, Lucien stared down at their sleeping baby daughter cradled in his arms.

Lucy was already three weeks old.

It had been the hardest and most wonderful three weeks of her life.

She was sleep deprived. Her breasts were aching. Sometimes she cried over nothing. But she was doing okay. It was still early days but Lucien's constant love and attention were helping her stay strong. She was minding herself too. Not stressing over the moments she felt down, accepting that all new mums did. Sleeping, eating healthily and exercising as much as she could. And most of all talking to Lucien. Reaching out to him and letting him into her thoughts and fears.

Her husband. Her daughter.

She felt complete.

She felt loved.

She felt safe and secure.

She knew just how lucky she was. To have met

a man who loved her so much. A man who, though apprehensive, had taken to fatherhood with enthusiasm and pride and love. A man who held her and whispered his love for her at every opportunity.

A man who had insisted that her parents move into the coach house for the entirety of Christmas. A man who had insisted on finding their Christmas tree himself and that they decorate it together while Lucy had slept in her downstairs cot. Christmas carols had played as he had cursed the lights that had become horribly tangled as they'd wrestled them onto the enormous tree that had had to be specially delivered by a delivery truck.

She stepped into the room.

His soft smile for Lucy grew even wider when he spotted her.

He beckoned her over with his eyes.

And when she was close enough he held out his hand to her and pulled her gently down onto his lap.

They smiled at each other.

And finally he whispered, '*Joyeux Noël*, Lottie.'

She rested her head against his chest. His lips touched reverently against her bed-head hair, as though he worshipped everything about her. And then he whispered, playfully, wickedly, 'Next time I know it will definitely be a boy.'

* * * * *